PAYING THE PRICE

Rachel Bowden, the illegitimate daughter of John Pearson, only learns of her father's duplicity as her mother lies dying. It transpires that both women came second to John's legitimate family – a bitter revelation that Rachel can neither forgive nor forget. Adopting a new identity as Lorna Daniels, she sets out to destroy John Pearson's other family. As Rachel slowly loses her grip on reality her crimes escalate out of control and it becomes a race for the police to find and stop her – before murder becomes the final act in her own personal revenge tragedy.

PAYING THE PRICE

PAYING THE PRICE

by

Janie Bolitho

Magna Large Print Books
Long Preston, North Yorkshire,
BD23 4ND, England.

British Library Cataloguing in Publication Data.

Bolitho, Janie
    Paying the price.

    A catalogue record of this book is
    available from the British Library

    ISBN   0-7505-2209-7

First published in Great Britain in 2003 by
Constable, an imprint of Constable & Robinson Ltd.

Copyright © 2003 Janie Bolitho

Cover illustration © Anthony Monaghan

The right of Janie Bolitho to be identified as the author of this work has been asserted by her in accordance with the Copyright, Designs and Patents Act, 1988

Published in Large Print 2004 by arrangement with
Constable & Robinson Ltd.

Magna Large Print is an imprint of Library Magna Books Ltd.

Printed and bound in Great Britain by
T.J. (International) Ltd., Cornwall, PL28 8RW

Janie Bolitho died from cancer
on 27th September 2002.
This book is dedicated by
her family to her loyal readers.

Chapter One

January 2000

Rachel Bowden had reached the age of twenty-five the previous day but there had been no birthday celebrations to mark the quarter-century. Her few remaining friends had tried to persuade her that it wouldn't hurt to miss one night and that they wanted to buy her a drink and a meal. Now she sat by the high-sided hospital bed holding a thin, dry hand as she listened at first with disbelief and then with fury to what Paula Bowden was telling her in a breathless voice.

Rachel's mother had been unwell for many years but the wasting disease from which she suffered had finally taken hold and her body was breaking down rapidly. Rachel no longer suspected but now knew for certain the reason for the acceleration. 'It's late. I'll come back in the morning,' she said through the lump in her throat, the lump which always preceded the tears of grief which she had, in advance and privately, already started to shed. Tonight they were caused by the pain of betrayal.

She left the over-heated hospital with its

now familiar smells and stepped out into the freezing night, catching her breath as the coldness filled her lungs. She passed wine bars and restaurants and Asian shops which opened late. Their bright displays of fruit and vegetables and materials shot with silken threads were set out on open stalls on the pavement, myriad colours gleaming joyfully beneath neon and sodium lights. They made a mockery of what was happening in that clinical hospital room.

The flat was not far from the hospital. It was large and warm and comfortable, one of six in a purpose-built block with a janitor and a regular maintenance service. The deeds were in her mother's name and until his disappearance the bills had been paid by Rachel's father. Paula had waited for his return until all hope had disappeared and then she gave in to her illness. At the time she had told Rachel that she had contacted the police but they were unable or unwilling to trace him. Tonight she had denied doing so.

Since her mother's rapid decline over the past year Rachel had hardly left the flat. She had taken indefinite leave from work to nurse her until there was no alternative but admission to hospital. That's how close they had been; how close she thought they had been.

Soon she must return to work, their

savings were running out. But her skills were in great demand, her job would be waiting – or another just like it.

Sleep was out of the question. She made tea but didn't touch it then poured a whisky which she did drink. And then another.

By the time what passed for winter daylight was showing around the edge of the curtains Rachel had come to a decision. She knew exactly what she had to do.

Showered and dressed and marginally less ragged for the coffee and toast she had forced herself to eat, she made her way back to the hospital. Her mother's face was paler still and sometime in the night she had been hooked up to various monitors. Rachel reached once more for that thin, dry hand and held it all day and into the early evening until the graph on a screen stopped flickering up and down and the bleeping green light on another gave one, long monotonous tone.

'Fifty-five, that's all she was,' she said to the nurse who tried to console her with tea. 'She told me things last night, things I'd never have guessed at. How can that be? Why didn't she tell me before?'

The nurse saw the desperate appeal in her eyes but there were no answers. She patted Rachel's shoulder and sighed. Deathbed confessions were all very well for the dying, but the damage they did to the living could be incalculable.

Chapter Two

July 2002

'Well, it's that time of year. Most people prefer to get married in the summer,' Moira Roper said as she looked up at her husband. Ian was scowling in the direction of the photographer, who was busily organizing people into groups. The wedding service had not gone on as long as he had feared, not like that of his son, Mark, who had married a French girl and done the whole bit in Rheims. 'For God's sake, smile, Ian, or at least take that awful expression off your face. You look more like your father every day.'

A comment which was enough to make Detective Chief Inspector Roper relax his facial muscles instantly even though his father was long dead.

'She's always been stunning but today she looks almost unbelievably lovely,' Moira said, unable to prevent an untypical romantic streak from surfacing.

'Not as good as you did.'

It was said quietly, almost gruffly, but Moira was touched. The man she had married all those years ago, the only son of strict, elderly parents, a man some years her senior, very rarely acknowledged aloud just how much he loved her. This was the nearest he came to it. And she still looked good. Without vanity she was aware that she had inherited her mother's fine bones, slender figure and pale blonde hair.

It was stifling in the churchyard. The grass was yellow and scratchy and in need of a cut, the carved words on the tombstones weathered and barely legible beneath lichen, but many of the weddings of the town took place at St Luke's because it was convenient, situated at the top of the High Street. Although it now nestled amongst supermarkets and a car park, there was a lych gate from which the bride and groom could be photographed.

Cigarettes were lit as the guests waited while the main party was arranged in staggered tiers and the small bridesmaids were persuaded to stand still. The pungent smoke of a cigar drifted visibly in unfelt air currents. Then, once the photographer had arranged the whole party to his satisfaction and fired off several shots, they were free to make their way to their cars and follow the newly married couple to the Duke of Clarence where the reception was being held.

Detective Constable Brenda Gibbons,

very recently made up to Detective Sergeant Gibbons, now had another change of title to which to adapt. Mrs Andrew Osborne. She had finally agreed to marry the man with whom she had had a long-standing relationship and with whom she had lived for nearly two years. He was a local solicitor, referred to by Ian as the ugly brute.

'Thank you for coming,' Brenda said as she passed him, radiant in shimmering white, her auburn hair cascading down her back beneath the turned-back veil.

Ian nodded. He wanted nothing more than to be out of the blazing heat which was causing his shirt to stick to him beneath his jacket and sink the first of what he hoped would be many pints of the local Adnams beer.

The bridal car pulled away. More cigarettes were lit and small cliques gathered. 'Come on, let's move.' Ian took Moira's hand and led the way. The Duke of Clarence was within walking distance and Ian had no intention of driving that Saturday, especially as he had all of Sunday in which to recover.

He suffered the glass of champagne they were handed upon entering the elegant hotel then, having exchanged the few required pleasantries, did as many of the male guests were doing, went straight to the bar. 'Dry white for me, please,' Moira said as she straightened her hat and glanced

14

around. Aware of Brenda's history, she knew that most of the guests were Andrew's friends or people Brenda knew from work. Her miserable past had allowed her few friends. Moira grimaced and prodded Ian. Scruffy Short was heading towards them, an amazing creature clinging to his arm. She was taller than him and plump with a mass of hair, the redness of which owed nothing to her genes. A shiny emerald green dress clung to her body and the heels of her white stiletto shoes seemed too thin to bear her weight.

'I thought I'd give Nancy an airing,' he said. 'Does her good to get out once in a while.' No introduction, no clue as to who the woman might be: sister, cousin, lover. Moira correctly guessed her to be the last. 'Meet my boss, Ian Roper, and his lovely wife, Moira.'

'Hi.' As Nancy extended a multi-ringed hand they were enveloped by heady perfume.

Moira hid a smile. Whoever Nancy was she was the ideal partner for Detective Inspector John Short.

Four and a half hours later Moira was in the hotel reception ordering a taxi home. Ian was drunk, there was no other word for it, as were many of the guests who had gone to town once Brenda and Andrew had sensibly left. And I'm not far off it myself, Moira realized. Her face was burning and her flimsy pale blue dress felt limp and crushed. Her hat was somewhere on a seat. It was time to get Ian home before he made a complete fool of himself in front of his fellow officers although it was doubtful if any of them would recall events from now onwards. Amazingly, Scruffy Short was still on his feet, as was Nancy.

'Great do,' Ian said with a little belch as he slid clumsily into the back of the cab. 'Great new start for our Brenda.'

Moira said nothing. Although Ian had grumbled for two solid weeks about giving up a Saturday for a wedding, she knew that he had enjoyed it and that he really was pleased for Brenda who, in earlier years, had survived an absent father, an alcoholic mother and a violent husband whom she had finally divorced. No wonder she had wanted a white wedding after the first disaster, which had been legalized in a register office. Fortunately the new vicar was open-minded about marrying divorced couples. No doubt he was pleased to get anyone into the church. Now Brenda had her promotion and a husband in the gentle likeable person of Andrew Osborne who may not have been blessed with good looks but was worth a dozen other men. He could not help his shambling gait or the pock-marks, a residue of teenage acne, which scarred his face but which he had not

16

allowed to sour his nature.

Back inside 14 Belmont Crescent Moira opened all the windows and the kitchen door to let out the stuffy air and a blow-fly which was banging itself against a pane of glass. It was still hot enough to sit in the garden in which she spent much of her spare time working. She sighed as she heard the clunk of the fridge door. Ian was pouring more beer. She might as well join him.

'I'll just have this then order us a Chinese. Wha'dya think?' he asked with a slight slurring of the sibilants.

It didn't matter what she thought. When Ian was in this sort of mood there was no point in arguing. She knew perfectly well that by the time the takeaway was delivered he'd be sound asleep in his chair.

Too hot and tired to bother with watering the runner beans, Moira lay back on the sun lounger and thought back over the day. A wedding was always the bride's day no matter what anyone thought, the one day upon which so many built their hopes. As if a beautiful dress, a church service and a cake could make any difference to what lay ahead. In Brenda's case the marriage stood more chance of working than many others. Although they had both been married before, they had matured and learned from their mistakes. She hoped they would be very happy. How many other marriages have taken place all over the country today, all over the world, in fact? Moira wondered as she felt her eyelids begin to droop and realized that she was in danger of spilling her wine.

Forty minutes later the front doorbell disturbed her. She paid the delivery man then placed the brown paper carrier bag in the kitchen. As she had known he would be, Ian was sound asleep, his hair tousled, his shirt unbuttoned and his mouth agape. At least for once he wasn't snoring.

Chapter Three

Earlier that same Saturday, seventy-odd miles away, another family was gathered. Beneath the formal clothing Robbie Pearce was sweating. This was partly because of the heat which had even penetrated the stone building of the church but mainly from an attack of nerves. He tried to concentrate on nothing but the dust motes which hung in the slices of sunlight streaming through the stained-glass windows. Don Shearwood, a friend since university days, had taken charge of his top hat and had the ring safely in his pocket. Don's wife sat in the second pew back on the right of the aisle, heavily and healthily pregnant. Despite the organist, the flowers whose scent filled the church and the full wedding regalia there were not that many guests.

The mechanism of the church clock whirred before it struck three. The bells began to ring. People coughed and shuffled in their seats and turned their attention to the Order of Service. Robbie glanced over his shoulder to the open doorway at the back of the church although he knew that when Lorna appeared the organist would see the vicar's signal in the mirror placed strategically beside him and the vaguely doleful music they were listening to would change to the stirring Mozart piece Lorna had chosen.

At five past three Robbie was impatient but unconcerned. Brides were traditionally ten minutes late and the photographer might be making a meal of it outside.

Ten minutes later, the bells still ringing, the vicar, who had been waiting just inside the open doorway, disappeared into the churchyard. The congregation no longer whispered but spoke in normal voices.

At twenty past three Robbie began to panic. There had been an accident; Lorna's car had not turned up; something unimaginably worse had happened. And where was Phillip, his mother's boyfriend, who was giving Lorna away because she had no relatives of her own and had considered her male friends to be too young for the job? He could hear the chatter of the bridesmaids and the page from outside the church. The former were his cousins' children, the latter was Don's small son. But where was Lorna?

The vicar approached the altar praying that what he feared had happened was not really going to be the case. He had had no experience in dealing with a last-minute change of mind. Perhaps the bride was simply being unreasonably selfish in delaying the ceremony.

There was a noise at the back. All heads turned as Phillip Hardy, flustered and sweating, rushed down the aisle. Alone.

'Oh, God, Robbie, you're not going to believe this.'

Robbie didn't. Nor did anyone else when they had left their seats and crowded around to hear what he had to say. Robbie nodded and hoped he wouldn't make an even bigger fool of himself by crying, which is what he felt like doing.

Anna Pearce, Robbie's mother, horrified and heartbroken on behalf of her son, saw that someone had to take charge of the situation. Everything had been paid for, by herself and Robbie. The guests had come expecting food and drink after the service; some had come a long way and were staying overnight.

'No, count me out,' Robbie said when Anna suggested they all go to the hotel anyway 'I couldn't face it, Mum, honestly I couldn't.'

She nodded. It had been a stupid suggestion. 'Just a minute, I'll have a word with the vicar.'

It was he who made the announcement that everyone was more than welcome to continue on to the reception. 'Mrs Pearce and Robbie would particularly like this rather than waste all the effort they've put into today,' he concluded.

The guests, stunned by events, filed slowly and silently out of the church. Some patted Robbie on the back and offered a few words of condolence on their way; others, far too embarrassed by the situation to know what to say to him, simply tried to pretend he didn't exist.

'Come and use my telephone, you'll need to let the hotel know,' the vicar said to Anna. They would be expecting the bride and groom and immediate family to appear first and they ought to be warned not to produce the wedding cake.

Anna found making that brief telephone call one of the hardest things she had had to do in her life. Speaking the words aloud made it all the more real. 'What do you want to do, Robbie? You can't go back to the flat, not tonight. Come back with us for a couple of days.'

Anna, Phillip and Anna's mother had intended staying at the London hotel where the reception was being held, but now that was an impossibility. Robbie and Lorna had a room booked at an airport hotel to be close to Heathrow for their honeymoon flight in the morning. Their room, the flight and the holiday must now be cancelled. This time it was Phillip who offered to make the calls, telling the vicar he was more than happy to pay for them.

'Good heavens, no, I wouldn't dream of it.' He was as shocked as everyone else had been but gratified to note that those whom it had affected the most were still able to act with dignity and politeness.

The drive from London to Rickenham Green was conducted almost in silence. Robbie and Audrey Field, his maternal grandmother, sat in the back of the car; Anna was next to Phillip who drove.

It was a scorching summer's day and the roads were busy with Saturday traffic. People were now returning home from wherever it was they went on a normal summer Saturday. To Robbie Pearce very little would ever again seem normal.

By the time they drove through the centre of Rickenham Green the shops were closed and one side of the street was in shadow. The sets of traffic lights were with them as they headed down Saxborough Road and out towards Little Endesley where both Anna and Audrey lived, although not in the same house.

Phillip turned into the driveway of Mulberry Cottage, a misnomer some predecessor had given the large, square, stone-built house which now glowed warmly in the evening sun. The scent of jasmine and honeysuckle filled the air and bees flew back and forth in the shiny leaves of the escallonia hedge which still bore numerous pink flowers.

Anna unlocked the front door. The marble-floored hall was cool and quiet but it felt as though she had been away for weeks not hours. She could smell the roses which were beginning to shed their petals around the base of the vase in which they were arranged, and a hint of the lavender polish she had used the previous day – it now seemed a lifetime ago. The grandfather clock ticked away the seconds they needed in which to compose themselves before anyone was capable of rational speech.

'Tea, or something stronger?' Phillip asked. He felt just as at home in Mulberry Cottage as he did in his own place. He was an estate agent and had sold the house to Anna and John over twenty-five years ago when he was a young man and his father had been head of the business.

'Whisky for me. A stiff one, please.' Anna took off her hat.

'And for me.' Audrey's face was very pale. She walked down the hall and entered a door to her right.

'Robbie?' Phillip waited. Robbie, even whiter than his grandmother, stared into space.

'Anything. Whatever we've got. I'm going to get very drunk tonight. But first I'm going to get out of these fucking ridiculous clothes.' He ran up the stairs to his old room where he kept some casual clothes for the

24

occasional weekends he spent with his mother. The top hat, he realized, must still be on the front pew of the church unless the vicar or Don Shearwood had rescued it. Don had wanted to come back with them but Robbie had turned down the offer.

They sat in the spacious sitting-room at the back of the house. Anna had opened the french windows. It was a perfect summer evening; from outside nothing but birdsong could be heard, inside there was only the chink of ice against the side of the glass which held Robbie's huge vodka and the fizz of dry ginger in Scotch as Phillip poured Audrey's drink.

Robbie had returned dressed in jeans and a T-shirt. His dark hair, so like his father's, was cut short in the modern style. His face was as pale and impassive as marble. Anna studied him, wondering if any clue had been given, any hint dropped that all was not well. She had found it unusual but not particularly odd that Lorna had chosen Phillip to give her away. Lorna's parents were dead, there was no other family and Phillip, to whom she had taken immediately, had been the ideal choice. 'Have you any idea at all why she's done this?' If Lorna was ill or in hospital she or someone would have let them know. Besides, she had telephoned Robbie the previous night and nothing had been wrong at that point.

'None whatsoever. Mum, I don't want to talk about it, not tonight. I can't even think straight let alone analyse what might have happened.'

He should be cutting the cake with his bride about now, Audrey was thinking, unable to imagine how it must feel to be in his position when he so clearly loved the girl. Audrey knew how lucky she was to have had a long and happy marriage until death had taken Bertie from her several years ago.

Audrey went to her daughter's kitchen and made sandwiches which no one ate. The bread curled at the edges as they sat with their drinks, each deep in thought and with no idea how to comfort Robbie.

Lorna had been to the house on many occasions. It seemed impossible they had all been so wrong about her, the lovely, laughing girl who had helped with the dishes and fitted in so well, who had spent hours at Audrey's cottage listening to her stories from the past. Anna squeezed her head between her thumb and middle finger. A headache was developing. It probably wasn't wise to drink but right then she needed another one. What to do now? Nothing, Anna realized. There was nothing that could be done except to allow for time to heal Robbie's wounds.

At nine o'clock Phillip walked Audrey home. It had been a long and upsetting day for her. 'No, darling, I need my own bed tonight,' she said when Anna suggested she stayed the night.

Robbie went up to his room but they guessed he wouldn't sleep much, if at all.

In the morning Anna grilled bacon and tomatoes and scrambled some eggs. They were hungry, they had eaten so very little yesterday, and now nature was taking its course. Robbie looked tired but not ill, as he had done the day before. Phillip and Anna had not slept much either. They had talked until late into the night, resolving nothing.

'I'm going to find her,' Robbie said as he picked up his knife and fork. 'I'm going to find her if it's the last thing I do. If nothing else, she owes me an explanation.'

Phillip and Anna exchanged a glance. It was doubtful whether he would succeed, and if he did nothing would be achieved except more heartache. But neither of them wanted to dampen his spirits, which had risen with this resolution: it would have been too cruel.

Chapter Four

Unlike Ian and Moira Roper the Pearce family did not enjoy the weekend. They each privately wondered if there was any possibility of ever enjoying anything again.

'But how on earth will you go about it?' Anna asked when Robbie reiterated his intention of searching for Lorna. They were picking at a late Sunday lunch which no one really wanted.

Robbie squinted as the afternoon sun reflected off the silverware on the dining-room table. Anna had high standards; the lovely detached house was beautifully kept, its traditional lines and furnishings a pleasure to live amongst. And so very different from Lorna's house although that was equally lovely. The house. Of course. That was the logical place to start. 'I'll go back to where she told me she lived,' he said.

'Why don't you stay a couple more days?' Anna reached for his hand.

'I've got to face the flat at some point. The sooner the better, I think.' The flat, where he had spent so many nights with Lorna. And being alone would give him a chance to get his thoughts in order, to try and see a way into the future. He had not expected the pain to feel so very physical, the ache for Lorna's touch to be so acute. And watching Phillip, so attentive towards his mother, he felt a pang of envy at the security of their relationship. Phillip would never let Anna down. They had been friends for many years, since his parents moved up from London and purchased the house via his estate agency. That was the year Robbie had been born. He had known no other home until university and, afterwards, the London flat that had been his father's.

After they had scraped the uneaten food from their plates and washed up they walked slowly down to the village. It was marginally cooler as they passed beneath the umbrella of the overhanging trees but they emerged once more into bright sunshine. They chose a table in the garden of the pub looking like any other family on a Sunday evening. Anna tried to ignore a couple who kept glancing pointedly in their direction. Most of the locals knew Robbie and therefore knew of the wedding. 'They've got to know at some point,' he'd said when Phillip asked if it was a good idea to go to the local pub. 'Anyway, I'm going back tomorrow. They can talk about me all they like once I've left.'

Anna had not liked to ask how he would spend the rest of his holiday. Possibly he'd change his mind about finding Lorna and decide to return to work.

'I'll go and see Grandma before I leave.' She had taken it badly, he knew that. If she thought he was coping she might feel better. Her dream had been to live long enough to have great-grandchildren That dream had been put on hold indefinitely now. He loved Audrey, just as he did his mother. Perhaps being such a well-adjusted family made what had happened seem worse. The people he knew didn't let each other down.

For the first time since he was ten and he had found his pet rabbit dead in its hutch, Robbie cried himself to sleep.

Audrey was dead-heading the roses in the front garden when Robbie pushed open the gate on Monday morning. From beneath the brim of her straw hat she studied him and saw the ravages in his face, but she realized he had come to reassure her. She wished she could hold him and rock him as she had done when he was small. But the pain he felt now was adult pain not that of a grazed knee or a bump on the head. Only he could deal with it this time.

Robbie kissed her cheek and tried to smile. 'The garden looks lovely.'

'It certainly keeps me busy. Come inside and we'll have some coffee.'

'I'm going back this afternoon.' He followed her to the tiny kitchen at the back of the cottage. The flagged floor helped to keep it cool. A gammon joint was simmering on the cooker. The rich, meaty smell made Robbie feel nauseous. He knew life had to go on and that his grandmother always cooked when she was upset but the idea of food was still repellent.

'So soon?'

'It's for the best.'

'Maybe.'

'I rang the local police this morning. I thought they might be able to suggest ways of trying to find her. I have to do it, Grandma, I have to know.'

'Oh?' Audrey hoped his mission would not become an obsession but she greatly feared that it might.

'I explained that Lorna wasn't local but that she'd been down here on visits, just in case anyone had seen her, I suppose.' He shrugged. 'Then I told them what happened on Saturday.' He took the cup and saucer Audrey handed him with shaking hands. She only drank instant coffee, claiming the real thing gave her stomach ache. 'The man I spoke to – a detective, actually – sounded sceptical. He said there was nothing they could do since no crime had been committed and she's not a juvenile. He asked if I'd thought about hiring a private detective.'

'And have you?' Audrey noticed he was avoiding using Lorna's name.

'No. I'll have a go myself first. I mean, no one can disappear without trace and there's her job and everything. That's why I want to get back. The sooner I start the more chance there is of finding her.'

Half an hour later Audrey watched him walk away. It seemed no time since she and Anna had travelled to Leeds for his graduation ceremony. How proud they had both been, prouder still when he'd got a job with a merchant bank ahead of several other candidates. 'He might look like John but he's got your analytical mind,' she had said to Anna some time ago. It had always been obvious that Robbie would end up working in the commercial world, even more so when his chosen subjects at university were economics and politics. John had been involved in the art world. Based in London during the week, he also travelled abroad to value items. His opinion was greatly sought after, his services always in demand, until a massive heart attack had killed him in the kitchen of Mulberry Cottage.

And now Anna has Phillip, for which I am truly grateful, Audrey thought as she picked up the secateurs from the garden bench. She had been aware of Phillip's feelings for her daughter long before he had surprised Anna by expressing them himself two years previously. As she worked she prayed that Robbie would also manage to find happiness for a second time.

Robbie had no luggage and no car as he had not been expecting to be at his mother's. His suitcase, packed for his honeymoon, was at the flat, in the hall, along with Lorna's. Of course, he thought with sudden optimism, she would have to return to collect it.

He was travelling back in his jeans. His wedding suit, hired from a shop in Rickenham in order that his mother could return it on Monday when he was off on his honeymoon, had disappeared from his room. The white shirt he had worn on Saturday was in the laundry basket but he would never wear it again.

Anna and Phillip waved as he went off in a taxi. He was catching a train from Rickenham but had refused the offer of a lift. He hated airport and station farewells. Phillip had taken the day off work knowing that Anna might need him. Justin would ring him at Anna's if there were any problems. Tomorrow they must all try and revert to normal.

Robbie was early. There were fifteen minutes to kill before the connection to Ipswich was due from where he would catch the London train. He sat on a seat on the almost deserted platform from which the heat rose in waves. A blackbird trilled in a tree and butterflies swarmed over the buddleia which grew wild and untamed behind the palings enclosing the small branch-line station. He got out his mobile phone, redialled the last number he had rung and asked to speak to Detective Sergeant Grant. 'Look, I don't want to seem a nuisance,' he began when he was put through, 'but is it possible for me to report Lorna Daniels as missing? I spoke to you this morning, if you recall.'

Gregory Grant suppressed a sigh. Robbie Pearce seemed to be under some sort of delusion. He had claimed to be jilted at the altar, if that phrase was still fashionable, at a wedding that was supposed to have taken place in London, so why call Rickenham Green? He also claimed his mother's lover had been to collect the bride from her house, again in London, only to discover she'd never lived there. The name Pearce meant nothing to Greg because he hadn't been in the area when John Pearce had been alive and a bit of a local celebrity.

The story sounded like an attention-seeking fantasy yet, even over the telephone, Robbie Pearce did not sound crazy. Desperate, yes, but not like some of the loonies who insisted upon speaking to someone in the CID. 'All I can suggest is that you report it to the police station nearest to where she … where she said she lived, sir, although I'm not certain they'll be able to do anything about it either.'

'Thank you. I'll do that. I'm on my way back to London now.'

Being conscientious, Greg Grant had made a note of the contents of the second call. If by any chance the body of a young woman should turn up it might be an aid to identification. Pearce had said there were no relatives, no one she might run to after a change of heart. The house bit was a mystery. He said he'd been there many times, but maybe he hadn't, maybe he had killed the girl and wanted to be caught but couldn't bring himself to confess. To cover himself Greg ran a quick check but no one by the name of Lorna Daniels lived in Rickenham Green or any of the surrounding villages.

Chapter Five

'Great do, wasn't it?' Detective Inspector John Short sat with his feet on the desk. In front of him was a container of milky coffee and a half-eaten cheese and pickle roll. These items comprised his breakfast.

Detective Constable Alan Campbell, who had also been at Brenda's wedding, nodded even though it had reminded him of his own marriage. Helen had been the only one for him until he discovered her secret sideline, a lucrative career as a pornographic film star. He was now divorced.

'You dour Scotsmen are all the same. No sense of fun, that's your trouble. Must be living in the shadow of all those mountains that makes you so miserable. You're in East Anglia now, boy, where everything's flat. Cheer up, for God's sake!' Getting no response Scruffy Short flicked through his in-tray. It had been a quiet weekend by normal standards. The heat was a funny thing: it could induce frayed tempers, especially when aided by the effects of alcohol, or, conversely, it could cause ennui, sapping energy, which is what seemed to have happened over the last couple of days because there was nothing in the night log, nothing in the morning's briefing and nothing on his desk to cause him to leave it, which was exactly the way he liked it.

The Chief Inspector was holed up in a meeting, the lovely Brenda Gibbons was away getting a leg-over and therefore offered no pleasurable distraction, and there were two detective constables and a sergeant to deal with anything which might crop up. John Short sipped his coffee and thought of Nancy of the dimpled thighs and how their Saturday night had ended.

DC Eddie Roberts, family man and conscientious worker, was going through the old unsolved crimes on files that were still open, albeit cold, theft being the most prominent. Maybe from a distance he might come across something they'd missed, some hallmark of a particular known criminal perhaps. No patterns were emerging but Alan would have already checked that.

DC Alan Campbell was busy at the computer, compiling statistics, which everyone knew were worthless but which red tape demanded of them, and Gregory Grant, the Sergeant and their newest member, was trying to hold a telephone conversation with what, judging by his changing facial expressions and the few comments he was able to make, had to be a nutter. They got their fair share of calls from those.

All neat and ship-shape, Short decided. A nice easy day ahead. And, apart from the nutter who rang again in the afternoon, it was.

DCI Roper, not fully recovered from the excesses of Saturday's wedding, was also pleased that no crimes warranting their attention had been committed over the weekend and that he was able to get away early.

The police station was in a three-sided precinct, the fourth side being the road. Modern office blocks were set around a fountain and several trees which had managed to survive despite their coating of dust and diesel. Ian walked around to the back of the station to his reserved parking space and wondered if this was the lull before the storm.

He drove home through the slow-moving five o'clock traffic and let himself into the house. Moira, who worked in the office of a garage showroom, wasn't yet home. Nor would she be for some time, he remembered, as she was having a night out with Deirdre, one of her oldest friends. He would have to fend for himself, something he had become accustomed to doing on odd occasions.

Unsure of the wisdom of his action he poured a glass of beer and took it out to the garden. The sky remained cloudless with no sign of the rain which had been forecast. He could smell the warm dryness of the soil and the nicotiana plants which grew beneath the window. As dusk descended and midges began to bother him, Ian went inside and got himself something to eat.

When Moira returned they sat drinking tea until late. Just as he was falling asleep Ian heard the ominous siren of a fire engine, closely followed by another. He opened his eyes, squinted at the LED display on his clock and groaned. It was almost one o'clock. Some damn fool's been careless, he thought, aware of how dry everything was because of the heatwave. He closed his eyes again and gave it no more thought until the morning when the fire officer's report was handed to him.

'This was a deliberate act of arson. The garage, a wooden structure, had been soaked in petrol then set alight. We got there in time to save the house. I think this is one for you, Ian.' The fax on top of the report was signed Gary French. Ian had worked with him on other cases.

Little Endesley. Was that where the engines he'd heard late last night had been heading? The fire department would make their own investigations but arson was a serious criminal offence. Gary French's report had also stated that the owner of the property was lucky, that if there had been more of a breeze or the neighbour hadn't spotted the flames in time the fire would certainly have spread to the house.

'Alan? Do us a favour? Have a look at any recent arson cases in our area, solved or otherwise, and let me have all the details.'

'Yes, sir.'

Ian stood with his hands in the pockets of his trousers and looked down on the street, now busy with shoppers. The general office, from which the detectives worked, was on the first floor. It was quiet and certainly not as decorative without the presence of Brenda Gibbons. Osborne, Ian reminded himself, her name is Osborne now. She'd be back next Monday because Andrew had a big case on during that week but they had planned a longer holiday for later in the year.

He turned to face the room, his six-feet-four-inch frame blocking the light from the window. He ran a hand through his thick, springy hair which was greying at the temples. He could – and should – have sent a DC out to Little Endesley but the sight of Scruffy Short with his straggly, nicotine-stained moustache and his crumpled clothing irritated him. And how the man imagined combing strands of hair over the dome of his head could disguise his baldness was a mystery to Ian. Inspector Short could get off his fat backside and do something useful.

Having been handed the details he read them. 'Will I find him at home or in his office?' Observing the Chief's stern expression, he thought better of suggesting that either Eddie or Greg went in his stead.

'The office. He's gone in to work. There's nothing he can do until the fire department's finished and our SOCOs have taken a look.'

Short picked up his notebook and keys and made his way downstairs. The minute he stepped out of the air-conditioned building sweat broke out on his forehead. He wiped it away with the sleeve of his jacket. Ten forty. What on earth would it be like by midday? They were just a bit too far away from Aldeburgh and Southwold to gain any benefit from whatever sea breeze there might be on the coast. At least the car, in its subterranean parking space, was cool.

He drove down Saxborough Road cursing the numerous sets of lights and finally reached the outskirts of the town. Here the houses were bigger; detached and hidden from the road behind high hedges. Once past them he turned left on to a B road and left most of the traffic behind him. Trees lined both sides of the road, their branches entwined overhead. The shadows of leaves dappled the bonnet, and the occasional shaft of sunshine pierced the summer density of the foliage and flickered across the windscreen. A mile further on he passed the sign for the village and slowed. Pulling into the side of the road he got out of the car and locked it then walked the few yards to Phillip's office.

The village was small; a few shops, a mini-supermarket, a post office which had managed to survive and two pubs. Second from the end of the little row of shops was Hardy's. Little Endesley seemed an odd location from which to operate an estate agency but there was a reason for this. It was the type of business which did not need a high street location; a family business, now in its second generation, Hardy's had gained a reputation. Everyone local knew where the office was and those further afield were easily able to find it through advertisements placed in national magazines and various other publications. The houses displayed in the windows were beyond most people's income. Short stopped to inspect them. Five-bedroomed detached residence with stables and three acres; converted barn with cobbled courtyard and swimming pool; old manor house in need of renovation; detached family home with magnificent views. The prices made him wince. All were a far cry from the modern box he inhabited but in which, despite its untidiness, or maybe because of it, he felt comfortable.

He pushed open the door. Surprisingly,

there was only one desk, behind which sat a serious-looking young man with spiky hair and John Lennon glasses. He stood up and smiled. 'Can I help you?'

'Inspector Short. Rickenham Green CID. I've come to see Mr Hardy.'

The young man, Justin Brown according to the nameplate on his desk, stared at Short's identity in a way which suggested he had never had any dealings with the police before, or none who had looked like Inspector Short. 'He's expecting you. He's in his office. I'll let him know you're here.' He went to the back of the room and opened the door, said a few words, then beckoned to Short to come on through.

Phillip Hardy was on the phone. 'Don't worry. I'll see you later,' he said before he hung up and stood to shake Short's hand. 'Do have a seat. Would you like some coffee?'

'I wouldn't say no.'

Phillip poured two cups from the filter machine on a table at the side of the room whose back windows looked out across open fields where crops were ripening.

'Fine, upstanding young man, your Justin.'

'Ah, yes. Yes, he is.' Phillip Hardy wasn't sure if the tone was mocking. He had no idea that the Inspector thought and spoke in clichés.

'Now about this fire.' Short spooned sugar

into his coffee and stirred it noisily; silver against bone china, no expense spared for the clients. 'Is there anyone you can think of who might bear you a grudge?'

'Good heavens, no.'

Short saw that his surprise was genuine but wondered why the idea hadn't crossed his mind. He certainly had to be worth a bob or two.

Despite his general appearance, his lechery and his disinclination to put himself out, Short's colleagues begrudgingly accepted that he was a good detective, one who had earned his promotion. He had a way of appearing to do nothing while his brain was working overtime. Within seconds he had summed Hardy up. He was a type; everyone was a type of one sort or another to some degree. Public or good grammar school, accustomed to money but not shy of working for it, educated, probably listened to classical music and went to the theatre. Pleasant face, not quite handsome, polite, never been in trouble. Honest? He'd soon find out. 'No enemies then? Rivals in business, anything like that?'

'No. Nothing. I'm not sure why you're asking. I assumed it was a tramp, you see. Got in there and tried to light a fire to cook on or a cigarette. It wasn't until the fire officer told me... Well, I still can't believe anyone would do such a thing deliberately.'

Sheltered life, Short added to his list. People did far worse things than that deliberately. 'You realize the house could have gone up, too, and you with it?'

Phillip nodded, his face pale beneath his tan. 'And I didn't hear a thing. I knew nothing about it until the fire engines arrived. The garage is to the side of the house and my bedroom's in the front.'

Short frowned. 'A neighbour rang the emergency services at around ten to one. She'd smelled the smoke through her open bedroom window. You were already asleep by then, I take it?'

'Yes, long before that. We had, well, what I can only describe as an unusual and exhausting weekend. I was exceptionally tired.'

'We?'

'My girlfriend and I.'

Randy sod, Short thought enviously. Nancy had insisted upon kicking him out early on Sunday morning with the excuse that she had things to do. He knew better than to question her as to what they might be. 'I understood that you live alone.'

'Oh, I do. I'd been staying with her. I got back about nine thirty and went straight to bed. I can promise you, Inspector, I saw or heard nothing and I've no idea at all who would do such a thing.'

'Who knew you'd be at home?'

'Nobody in particular. I don't account for

my actions to my friends.'

'But your car wasn't there. It might've seemed as if you were still away.'

'My car's being serviced. I dropped it into the garage yesterday morning and got a taxi to bring me back here after I left Anna's house.'

'You're insured?'

'Naturally.'

There wasn't a flicker of panic or guilt but Short hadn't really expected there to be. Phillip Hardy did not come across as a man who would set his garage alight to claim a few quid. They would check his finances anyway. Fraud was also a serious crime. But it was obvious the man couldn't help them. 'If you think of anything unusual or anyone who might bear a grudge, let us know, even if it seems trivial to you.'

'Unusual?' Phillip smiled wanly. 'Life certainly seems to be that at the moment.'

'Oh?' Short was already on his feet ready to leave.

Phillip shook his head. 'Family troubles. Nothing to do with this, I promise you.'

'I'll see myself out. 'Bye.'

Driving back, Short wondered what sort of family troubles. According to their information Hardy lived alone, his wife had divorced him years ago and there were no children. Gary French had made their lives a little easier by asking all the relevant questions. It was unlikely that a wife who had run off with someone else would wait fifteen years to seek revenge and there were no disgruntled or greedy offspring in the picture. So what family then? He kicked himself for not asking at the time.

'What did you make of him?' Ian chewed the end of a biro. He had been right. Things had been too quiet. Since Short's departure there had been a stabbing outside the Black Horse in Saxborough Road. A stabbing in broad daylight with plenty of witnesses at ten fifteen on a Tuesday morning. The victim and his attacker had both been drunk. The Black Horse was known for its fences and criminals and after-hours drinking but the police turned a blind eye for two reasons. Firstly they knew where to look for the villains and, secondly, it was also where some of their informants drank.

'Hardy? Straightforward, I'd say.'

'That's what French thought.' Hardy had been roused by the sirens. The driver of the first engine had seen the front upstairs light come on before Hardy appeared at the front door wearing a short, towelling bathrobe. The neighbour who had called them lived in another detached house some fifty or sixty yards to the rear of Hardy's property. When asked why she hadn't rung Hardy to warn him she had said she thought he was still away. She hadn't seen his car and there were no lights on in the house. 'And I assumed that if he was at home, he'd have noticed the flames or smoke himself,' she'd added.

'Possible motive?' Ian asked.

'None that's obvious at the moment.'

'Well, keep at it.'

Short nodded and went off to begin on the paperwork.

By four in the afternoon it was known that the stabbing victim was stable and would survive. The man who had lunged drunkenly towards him with the knife was in the cells sobering up. Neither of them were known to the police.

Having banked on another quiet day Ian had promised to take Moira out that evening. They'd have a couple of drinks in the Crown, Ian's favourite pub and not only because the landlord kept the Adnams in top-class condition, then go for a Chinese. There was one more job to do before he left. He needed to know if the man in the cells was up to answering questions yet. He picked up the phone and rang the custody officer.

'The Doc's just finished with him. Shall I send him up?'

'Please.'

Doc Harris had been to have a look at Dennis Suitor earlier when he was still out cold but had since returned. Jim Harris was a local GP who was on the rota of police surgeons, although as they were never required to perform surgery or post-mortem examinations he thought it rather a misnomer. 'He's all yours,' he told Ian when he came up from the cells. 'A serious case of the DTs, but otherwise okay.' He grinned. As old friends they had shared a few hang-overs themselves.

'"Otherwise okay"? That's a strange description. He stabbed someone.'

The Doc, rotund and far shorter than Ian, raised his greying head. 'Physically. You want a psychological report, get Brian Lord. Anyway, fancy a snifter tonight?'

Ian did not hesitate. 'No, not tonight, Jim. Later in the week, maybe.' A snifter was a euphemism for large quantities of single malt at the Elms Golf and Country Club where Jim was a member. Saturday wasn't far enough behind him yet to contemplate a night out with Jim. The Doc's second wife, Shirley, so very like Janet, his first, who had died, had endless tolerance where her husband was concerned and would drive out to collect him when necessary.

'Are you interviewing him yourself?'

'No, Eddie Roberts'll do it.'

'Ah, young Eddie and his brood. He's one of my patients.' Like everyone else Jim Harris knew that Eddie's house was always full of relatives from both sides of the family, a fact he neither resented nor

49

complained about. 'See you soon.' With a wave, he left the room.

There were witnesses who had seen the two men leave by the pub's side door and the actions which followed. Suitor had been so drunk he had staggered against the wall and fallen to the pavement where he remained until the police and an ambulance had arrived. Now that he was sober enough to understand what was going on he could be charged.

Eddie Roberts, brighter and less haggard now that his youngest child was sleeping through the night, whistled as he made his way down the corridor of interview rooms where Dennis Suitor and a uniformed PC awaited him.

Suitor was nervous. He fidgeted and, despite the air-conditioning, wiped his forehead with a tissue. He listened carefully as the procedure was explained. Next to him sat one of the duty solicitors.

Eddie ascertained his name, address, age, which was forty-one, and occupation and the fact that he had gone to the Black Horse on Monday night, but that was the extent of the information Suitor was able to provide.

'I can't remember leaving,' he said. 'I don't know what happened. The last I recall is Dave chatting to some woman.'

'Why were you carrying a knife?'

'It wasn't mine. I don't know where it

came from.'

'Are you married?'

'No. We split up about ten years ago.'

There had been nothing on Suitor to suggest who his next of kin might be so they had been unable to notify anyone of his whereabouts. And he hadn't been in a fit enough state to tell them who to contact, let alone make his permitted telephone call.

'Look, you have to believe me, I don't know what happened and that's the honest truth.'

'How well do you know Dave Johnson?'

'Fairly well. His wife and mine were friends, that's how we met.'

'Do you drink together often?'

'Now and then.'

'Why did you stab him?'

'Look, I really don't know. I can't believe I did it. What'll happen to me now?'

'My client needs a break,' the solicitor said, aware of what the answer would do to Suitor, and knowing that there was little to be said in his defence. Admitting to drunkenness was no protection from the law and he hadn't even tried to claim self-defence.

Eddie told the tape that the interview had ended and stated the time. Then he went upstairs to report to the Chief.

Suitor was taken back to his holding cell. He would appear before the court in the morning. If he was lucky he'd be released on bail.

'It seems fashionable this week, motiveless crime,' Ian said wryly when Eddie had finished. There was nothing new on the arson case and Phillip Hardy was now free to make his insurance claim and have his garage rebuilt. Hopefully, this time, with breeze blocks.

Ian quickly scanned Short's printed notes which told him nothing about Hardy and the fire he hadn't known before then made his way to the Crown where he'd arranged to meet Moira to save them both going home first.

He walked up the High Street, grateful for the light breeze which ruffled his hair, then turned into the alleyway which led to the Green. Here, low cottages were huddled around the grass in which stood an enormous oak surrounded by a slatted wooden bench. The Green once comprised the village which had gradually expanded into a large town.

Moira was at the bar talking to Bob Jones, the landlord, and his wife Connie. 'Mine's a pint,' Ian said, kissing her on the cheek and deciding to put work behind him for the evening.

'Honestly, no wonder they wind you up. You always seem to time your entrances perfectly.'

'A technique picked up only after years of practice. Come on, then, get your purse out, woman.' He grinned at Bob Jones who already had his pint poured and standing ready on the bar.

On Tuesday afternoon Phillip left work at the usual time of five thirty. After the visit from Inspector Short he had tried to settle into his normal routine. He had dealt with correspondence and shown a couple around the barn conversion which still smelled of new wood and gloss paint. They were interested, he sensed it, but he never pushed clients, that wasn't the way he, or his father before him, worked; he simply encouraged them.

Robbie had returned to London yesterday. Phillip was taking Anna out for dinner because neither of them felt like cooking and he didn't want Anna to sit and brood. Audrey had refused the invitation to join them.

Over the meal he told her about the fire, playing down the danger the fire officer had said he had been in. 'The police are investigating now,' he concluded.

'But you could have been killed,' Anna said, shocked, but reading between the lines. 'My God, Phillip, who would want to do such a thing?'

'That's exactly what the police would like

to know. I haven't a clue.'

Anna sipped her wine. 'Let's hope there isn't a third thing,' she said quietly.

Chapter Six

When Robbie had opened his front door late on Monday afternoon he had known what he would find there but he hadn't expected the impact that seeing Lorna's case would have upon him. It was akin to a physical blow to the guts.

Shaking, he had gone into the large room at the front and sat down. She had a key, he had half expected her to have taken her things during his absence. She would surely have guessed he had gone to Little Endesley. He poured a small whisky and sipped it slowly. Then he unpacked his own case, throwing the mocking shorts and beachwear to the back of the top shelf in his wardrobe. The fridge had been emptied prior to Saturday – he had not expected to be home for a fortnight – so he went out to buy milk and something he might be able to eat. Anna rang just after ten. He took the call, reassured her he was fine then went to bed where he slept restlessly.

Somehow he got through the night. On Tuesday morning, just before nine, when he couldn't wait any longer, he got into his car which he kept parked at the rear of the block of flats and drove from central London out to Ealing. It seemed to take for ever in the heavy morning traffic.

He had met Lorna a little under two years ago, soon after his mother and Phillip had got together. It had been a chance meeting at an art gallery. Without thinking Robbie had opened an invitation which had been addressed to his father. He had been dead for about four years by then and Robbie had not expected any more post to come for him. Seeing the name Pearce he had not taken any notice of the initial.

His father had died not long before his graduation so Anna had suggested, if he intended working in London, that he use the flat as his base. The deeds to the property had been her wedding present to them.

Lorna had been at the gallery. He never did find out how she had obtained an invitation to the preview. His father's had come from the Italian painter whose exhibition it was. Obviously he had not heard of John Pearce's death. It had been a shock to him when Robbie told him. 'I only met John a few times but I liked him so much. He had honour and integrity,' the painter told him. 'But I am proud to meet his son.' There hadn't been a chance to speak again because the artist had to mingle and then Robbie had stepped on Lorna's foot as he stood back to admire a painting. Later he had taken her to dinner.

He reached the quieter suburbs and pulled up outside the Ealing house he had come to know so well over the past year. It had been quite a while before Lorna had taken him there. From the outside it looked like any other in the pleasant terrace but she had done wonders with the interior. There were bare, polished floors, an open spiral staircase to the first floor and a kitchen which was all chrome and tiles and which should have looked clinical but didn't because of the collection of jugs lining the open shelves. And the flowers. There were always flowers. The whole effect was spartan, foreign somehow, but it felt like a home because of the personal touches and the predominance of books.

He took a deep breath and rang the bell. A woman in her sixties opened the door. She had grey hair and was a little untidy as if she hadn't long been up. Against the background of Lorna's choice of decoration she seemed incongruous. A cigarette burned in her hand.

'Good morning. My name's Robert Pearce. I know this is going to sound a bit strange but I'm trying to locate the previous owner of the house.'

The woman shook her head. 'I don't know what it is about this place, we haven't been here all that long but you're the second person to come looking for someone in the past couple of days.' She looked him up and down, took in the casual but smart clothes, the short, neat hair and the accentless voice and decided he was harmless. 'I'm Vi Baxter. You'd better come in.' Her own voice was pure East End.

He was shown into the living area to which, he was surprised to notice, no changes had been made. Mrs Baxter, so very unlike Lorna, obviously liked what had been done to the house and had decided not to change it. By why, oh why, had Lorna sold up and moved without telling him? And why had Phillip, on Saturday, been told that the Baxters had no knowledge of anyone called Lorna living in the house before they moved in? Robbie had been there many times, had slept in the bed which was a thick mattress on a raised dais in the middle of the main bedroom. Phillip had not had time to ask questions, he had had to return to the church with the news.

'Would you like some tea?' Vi Baxter found an ashtray and put out her cigarette. She knew that her husband would be back from the shops at any minute and the young man did not seem threatening.

'Yes, please.' The offer of tea meant she was prepared to sit and listen and, hopefully, to talk.

She wasn't long in the kitchen which he could visualize so clearly, the kitchen where he and Lorna had prepared meals together. He had to stop such memories from rising to the surface, they caused nothing but gut-wrenching pain and an unmanly desire to weep.

'Now, what's all this about?' Vi handed him a mug and indicated he help himself to sugar from the bowl on the tray. 'Some man was here on Saturday, all dressed up for a wedding. He'd come to collect the bride, he said. Well, I knew that wasn't me.' She laughed throatily before her face froze. She suddenly realized who Robert Pearce must be.

'Her name is Lorna Daniels. We were to have been married on Saturday. She didn't turn up. She lived here, you see, or so she told me.'

Vi shook her head and picked at a piece of fluff on her red polyester trousers. 'The woman we bought the house from was called Halmer. Ottie Halmer. She's German.'

'What did she look like?'

'Attractive for her age. Mid-fifties, I'd say. Shoulder-length blonde hair, decent clothes. She's some sort of medical specialist, not a doctor, I think she said she does some sort of research but I can't remember exactly. She'd got a three-year contract in the States. She told us she was selling up because she'd got no ties in England any more and she didn't want the hassle of letting because, if things turned out all right, she'd probably stay in the States.'

America. How on earth could he find anyone there? And no way could Ottie Halmer's description fit Lorna. 'Did you ever see anyone else here?'

'We only came the once. We knew immediately this was the place for us and we shook hands on it on the spot. Miss Halmer was leaving the curtains and all the fittings so there was no need to come back to measure up or anything.

'She was so pleased we wanted it, especially as we offered the full asking price. She'd been away, over in Germany, working and visiting her family. She only came back for a week. I suppose the estate agent held the key while she was away. There wasn't any board outside. Miss Halmer didn't want one. Some people don't, you know. It's not obligatory, apparently.'

'When was this?'

'When was what?' Vi Baxter reached for another cigarette.

'When you came to view the place.'

'Oh, back in March. We explained we didn't want to move until George retired. He's my husband. We haven't got a car, see, and he could walk to work from where we lived before.

'Anyway, she had to go back to Germany before she flew out to the States so this month suited both of us as a completion date.' She paused. 'I don't know where any of this leaves you, though. I certainly don't know anything about a Lorna. It couldn't have been her daughter, could it?'

Robbie shrugged. He didn't know. Anything was possible. 'You don't have a forwarding address for Miss Halmer, do you?'

'No, but I expect a lady like that would have made the necessary arrangements for her mail to be forwarded.'

'Mrs Baxter, would you be prepared to give me the name of the solicitors who did your conveyancing?'

'If it'll help, but I doubt they'd tell you where she is even if they know.' She got up. 'Ah, here's George.'

Robbie heard the front door close and muted voices in the hall and guessed his hostess was giving her husband a brief résumé of their conversation. She came back alone and handed him a piece of lined paper on which she had printed the name and address of their solicitors with a thick, felt-tipped pen.

'Thank you, I really appreciate this. I won't take up any more of your time.'

She saw him to the door. 'I hope you manage to get things sorted out,' she said, not knowing quite what else she could say.

Robbie walked to his car clutching the piece of paper, oblivious to the heat of the sun on his head and the dusty dryness of the foliage of the shrubs in front gardens. If he could just find Ottie Halmer he might have a chance of finding Lorna.

Dave Johnson knew he was due a visit from the police and was surprised he hadn't received one yet. He lay in his hospital bed wearing a ridiculous white gown with blue flowers because he didn't own any pyjamas and watched the doorway. Dave didn't remember the ambulance ride or anything much that had happened until he had woken from the anaesthetic. That had been about tea-time yesterday. Already he felt stronger and had been allowed to sit in the chair at the side of his bed while the nurses straightened his sheets. His injuries had not been as bad as initially suspected – he'd be home in a day or so, the doctor had told him.

The tea trolley had been around. Dave sipped a cup of something which was supposed to be coffee and tried to decide what to tell the police. The question was, what had Dennis told them? Dennis had been pissed, completely pissed, so hopefully he'd have total alcoholic amnesia. Dave decided to take a chance on it.

'The sister says we can talk to him,' DC Eddie Roberts told Ian. 'Want me to go, sir?'

'No, send Greg. You carry on with the arson inquiries.' Phillip Hardy's financial background was being investigated discreetly, although Ian was certain nothing untoward would be discovered. The family business was doing extremely well and from what he had heard of the man Hardy was respected as a straight dealer. His house was paid for, as was his car, he had only living expenses to worry about. And judging from the prices of the properties he sold, one sale a month at two and a half per cent commission, if that was the going rate, would bring in at least nine thousand pounds. There would be overheads – the premises, printing, postage and Justin's wages – but they would not amount to a great deal compared with a business where stock had to be bought.

The thought had crossed his mind that kids might have been responsible for the fire but Gary French, with whom he had now spoken over the phone, did not agree. 'Too good a job, Ian. From what we could make out all three walls and the door were soaked with petrol. Where would kids have got so much in Little Endesley? There's no garage. And apart from the petrol everything burned evenly so there was certainly more than one point of ignition. Youngsters would've thrown some matches and run. No, this was too well organized,' he had concluded.

And the scene-of-crime officers had found no evidence; no cigarette ends, no sweet wrappers, no spent matches, no petrol cans. Someone had been very careful. And, because of the heat wave, there were no tyre marks and no footprints in the unmade-up lane leading to the house. The wooden structure, also very dry, had burned quickly. Gary French was certain that the fire had been lit from the outside. Had the arsonist known the garage was empty? There might have been a car inside, possibly even a person – Hardy had said he didn't lock the garage when he was out, there was no point as he kept nothing in it.

'Sir?'

'Sorry, Eddie, I was thinking. If Greg's not busy ask him to get over to the hospital now. We don't want to give Johnson too long to think up a story.'

DS Gregory Grant, widowed and now living alone in a small house on the Bradley Estate, set off for Rickenham General. Thoughts of his wife no longer filled his head every minute of the day and night and he didn't know whether to feel grateful or guilty. His daughter, recently married, told him that this was natural, a gradual letting go. The move to a new area had done him good.

Rickenham General was inconveniently situated several miles out of the town. It was a vast, ugly building which served a wide area. It took him nearly fifteen minutes to find a parking space in the large complex and then he was nowhere near the ward he wanted. There were coloured lines next to the walls along the floors of the corridors. Having been told to follow the blue one he did so before stepping into the lift, rising five floors and following the line again. It led to the surgical wards. Dave Johnson was in Nightingale, an unoriginal name, Greg thought, as he stepped into the sister's office to explain who he was. Hospital smells didn't bother him, he'd lived with them long enough and, in fact, Nightingale ward smelled pleasantly of flowers.

'Fourth bed on the left,' she told him but made no further comment, either from lack of curiosity or because she had seen it all before.

The sallow-faced man was sitting up reading a newspaper but Greg knew he had seen him coming. He pulled out a chair and sat down.

'I was expecting you sooner,' Johnson said when Greg had introduced himself. 'What do you want to know?'

'What time did you go to the Black Horse on Monday?'

'Tennish. Monday night, that is.'

'And you stayed all night?'

'Yes, three or four of us.' Dave had no qualms about dropping the landlord in it, he could always claim it was a private party. It was himself he was worried about.

'And Dennis Suitor was with you all the time?'

'He was.'

'What was the argument about?'

'No good asking me. There was no argument. We were pissed, it's as simple as that. I knew I had to get myself home somehow and face the wife. I assumed Dennis would share a cab with me. We left just as Tony was cleaning up before the morning session.'

Greg had met Tony Peak, the landlord, during his first week in Rickenham when Eddie Roberts had taken him into the pub. 'I'll show you the sights,' Eddie had said. And Tony Peak was a sight. He weighed seventeen stone and had a mass of hair and a bushy beard. His trousers were hitched under his enormous stomach with an invisible belt and his white shirt was grubby. But Peak was a man to keep in with. Villains might use his pub but he had been a useful source of information. However, it was his small and skinny wife who ruled the roost.

'And for absolutely no reason Suitor stabbed you?'

'Yes.' He's lying, Greg thought but there was little he could do about it. Johnson might even refuse to go to court which would make their case hopeless.

'Did you know he had a knife?'

'He didn't. It was mine.'

It was said a little too quickly. 'Who was the woman with you?'

Dave Johnson looked surprised. 'What woman?'

'I understood you were talking to one.'

'I talk to lots of them, mate, it doesn't actually mean anything.'

'You said you were married.'

'Yes, but not so you'd notice.' He laughed. 'Do you think I'd have been out all night if there was something worth going home for? We do our own thing these days.'

'Are you sure you didn't say anything to upset Suitor?'

'As far as I know, the answer's no but like I said, we were both pissed.'

Greg nodded. The finality of his tone and body language told him that Johnson had adopted the attitude of 'That's my story and I'm sticking to it.' He stood, ready to leave. 'When are they discharging you?'

'Tomorrow or the next day. It wasn't as bad as they thought. No internal injuries, missed me vitals apparently, just a bit of needlework.'

'We'll be in touch.' Greg walked away. He was going to see Tony Peak but doubted he'd learn anything new there either.

The Black Horse was open although it was hard to tell from the outside. Yellowed nets hung at the windows and the dim lighting was not visible against the brightness of the street. Peak was behind the counter. Either he or his blowsy wife worked all the shifts; they seemed to have no other life than the pub.

The atmosphere was smoke-filled and moribund. There were several customers seated at the scarred tables. They studied papers or stared morosely at the drinks in front of them as if they were simply waiting for life to end when their troubles would be over. The carpet was sticky beneath Greg's shoes.

'Morning. What can I do for you?' Peak scratched his immense belly.

'Just a quick word, it won't take long.' So he recognized me, Greg thought. Not, What can I get you? but What can I do for you? 'Tell me what happened during the course of Monday night and Tuesday morning?'

'Monday was quite busy, don't ask me why. I closed up in the evening as usual and had a bit of a private do for some of my regulars. No more than half a dozen of them.' Greg wrote down their names, though sensing it was a pointless exercise. None of them would talk. 'The lads stayed the night and I opened up again in the morning and my wife took over so I could get some kip. I know what you're going to ask me but no, there weren't any arguments. Dave and Dennis left together. They'd had a few, more than a few, but there was no trouble in here. You can ask anyone.'

'Who was the woman they spoke to?'

'Now that's a mystery. Not our usual sort of customer. Nice-looking, youngish and well dressed. Spoke nicely, too. She came in, ordered a drink and sat over there in the corner. She had a second drink and when she came up for it that's when Dave spoke to her. No, wait, I think she spoke to him. Not that it matters either way, she left soon after that. Dave can't seem to help himself, any woman's game for him, not that his wife cares.'

'What did they talk about?'

'I didn't hear the beginning. He gave her a few chat-up lines, that's all I heard of the conversation. I had other customers to serve.'

'Did they talk for long?'

'Not more than a few minutes, I shouldn't think, because when I looked back her glass was empty and she'd gone. Can't say I blame her, who'd want to get involved with Dave?'

'What about Suitor, did he speak to her?'

'Not that I saw. He just nodded when she came up to the bar.'

So the argument, the non-existent argument, didn't seem to have been over a woman, a woman they had no chance of finding if she had wandered in there by chance before realizing what sort of place it was. Except, Greg thought as he thanked Peak and left, she had stayed for a second drink...

Ian was trying to get the barbecue going. It was not a task he enjoyed, nor was he very good at it – not that he had had much practice, given the unreliability of British summers. The heat wave had continued for over two weeks, the longest spell of sunshine he could remember. And this was why Moira had invited Doc Harris and Shirley and Deirdre and Peter over for the evening.

Deirdre, a friend of Moira's for as long as he could remember, had, like Jim Harris, lost her spouse at a young age. She had been on her own for far longer than she had been married. It had been a surprise to both of them when she announced she had met someone else. Deirdre's charitable works and her part-time job and her house and garden had always seemed enough for her. And Deirdre, as nice as she was, as much as Ian liked and respected her, could never have been described as attractive.

Moira had informed him that Peter taught games and what Ian had known as Divinity, although the subject now encompassed various religions. As Ian was agnostic and the only exercise he took was a stroll to the pub he felt sure he would dislike the man. Beard and sandals, he thought, earnest and politically correct, a touchy-feely, caring-sharing type. He smiled wryly at his prejudiced ideas. As a policeman he should know better than to prejudge anyone.

Jim Harris and Shirley appeared around the side of the house. 'Just in time,' Ian said. 'Here, you take over.' He handed the Doc some matches. In seconds smoke was rising from the coals.

'That calls for a drink, Chief Inspector,' Jim said, smiling at his own success.

Ian went to the small table upon which he had set out bottles and glasses. There was no need to ask what they wanted, he had known them far too long for that.

'And one for me, please,' Moira said as she appeared from the kitchen doorway with bowls of salad. The front doorbell rang. 'Oh, that'll be Deirdre.' She grinned, aware of how Ian pictured Peter whom he hadn't met.

Moira ushered the new arrivals into the garden.

'Ian, this is Peter, Peter, Ian. And Jim and Shirley.'

Peter extended his hand to Ian who frowned and then smiled. Deirdre had not worn well and looked older than her forty-five years. Even allowing for this Peter was obviously quite a bit younger than her. His jeans had a designer label on the back pocket and his casual open-neck shirt suited him perfectly. Tall and lean, he had a boyish face and short, spiky fair hair. 'Hi. I'm pleased to meet you at last.' He shook hands with Jim and Shirley and asked if Ian had any beer. 'Real ale. Marvellous,' he said, thus surprising Ian a second time when he produced a plastic bottle of Adnams.

'You teach, I believe.'

'Yes. And you police our streets, I hear.'

'I do.' He glanced over at Moira who ignored him and continued talking to her other guests before going to fetch bread and the meats for the grill. 'I couldn't do your job.'

'Likewise. Mind you, the brats drive us all around the bend. Some of them will end up coming to your attention. We have one in particular who seems to have a budding career as a pyromaniac. In his case it runs in the family. He's got a big brother who taught him all he knows.'

'Oh?'

'You might know of him already. Anyway, enough of work. Have you been watching any of the golf on the box?'

Ian wasn't sure whether the change of subject was because Peter Bennett realized he might be breaching some sort of confidentiality or because he really didn't want to talk about his work.

By the end of the evening he knew he had been completely wrong about the man. He was good company and made them all laugh. And he liked football. Ian made a point of seeing him and Deirdre to the door. There was no chance of the Doc going home for at least another hour.

'It's been a great evening. Thanks. And the food was terrific.'

'I'm glad you enjoyed it. Look, if you'll excuse the pun – I hope I'm not asking you to tell tales out of school, but can you give me the name of the family you were talking about earlier? The pyromaniacs. It might be relevant to something we're working on at the moment. If they're known to us, no harm will've been done, but if you'd rather not then I understand.'

Peter considered the question then nodded. 'The name's Jones. They live in the council houses at Little Endesley. Four boys and the mother. The last they heard of the father he was inside for theft. It wasn't the first time. Apparently this time he decided not to come home after he was released. It's the usual story, the boys don't really stand a chance.'

'Thank you.' Ian did not say that he would not reveal his source: Peter Bennett would take that as read.

The name Jones meant nothing, although

the boys' crimes may have been too trivial to have come to his attention. But they did live in Little Endesley which was where the blaze that destroyed Hardy's garage had been started.

'A successful evening, I'd say,' Moira commented as they cleared up rather later than they had anticipated. 'What did you make of Peter?'

'Don't smirk, woman. You know I liked him.'

'Not what you expected, huh?'

'Not at all.'

'Fancy Deirdre having a toy-boy,' he said later as he got into bed beside his wife.

'Toy-boy? Honestly, Ian, you really do date yourself sometimes.'

He grabbed her playfully. 'Date myself? Stop chattering and I'll prove there's life in me yet.'

Chapter Seven

Robbie took the precaution of telephoning the school secretary to make an appointment to see the headmistress. The summer holidays were only days away, and he assumed she would be busy with end-of-term activities. He had to wait until Thursday morning to speak to her in person. He wanted to watch her reactions to his questions, therefore a telephone conversation was not suitable for his purposes. Deep down he knew that he also wanted to be in the place where Lorna had worked, as if the building could give him some clue to her whereabouts.

He had already been to see Mrs Baxter's conveyancing solicitor at the poky offices from which she operated. Barbara Hughes turned out to be a plain and seemingly characterless person, albeit polite and helpful. She had listened to his explanation and sympathized with him. 'I can get the address from Miss Halmer's solicitor,' she told Robbie, 'but I won't be at liberty to give it to you. However, what I can do is to forward any letter you'd like to write.'

'Couldn't you telephone her? I'll pay any

costs, of course.' It would be days before the letter reached its destination and there would be a further delay in receiving a reply, if Ottie Halmer even bothered to put pen to paper.

'I could try, I suppose. But I can't ring now because of the time difference. Look, leave it with me, I'll see what I can do and I'll be in touch.' She wrote down the questions he needed answers to and hoped she could help him locate the girl. What neither of them knew was that Ottie Halmer was touring and visiting old friends prior to taking up her post in September. 'I'll need a number where I can reach you,' she had said, letting him know the session was at an end.

At ten thirty on Thursday morning Robbie sat in one of the three steel-framed chairs lined against the wall outside Janice Meek's office. A group of small, noisy, giggling children wearing blue polo shirts with the school's logo glanced at him inquisitively before entering a classroom door. The corridor had that particular odour common to all primary schools, a mixture of chalk, disinfectant and school dinners.

The office door opened. 'Mr Pearce? I'm Janice Meek, headmistress here. I'm sorry to have kept you waiting. Please come in.' She shook Robbie's hand with a firm grip.

She was younger than he had expected

and soberly dressed but her brown curly hair and wide smile softened the effect.

'My secretary said you wanted to see me about a member of the staff here. How can I help you?' He was just about old enough to be a father of one of the youngest pupils. She wondered what the problem could possibly be that demanded an urgent appointment.

'Yes. Her name's Lorna Daniels. She teaches, or taught, here until recently. We were to be married last Saturday but she didn't turn up at the church and somebody else has now moved into her house. I'm trying to find her. I need to know what's happened, you see.' It was becoming easier to say each time.

Janice Meek had not been expecting anything like this. 'How dreadful for you.' She saw the pain in his eyes and paused before letting him down. 'The thing is, Mr Pearce, no one of that name has taught here in my time and I've been here for a little over ten years.'

Another lie? It had to be. But Lorna had described the place so accurately, had even named the head teacher and other staff. And he had phoned her during her lunch hour occasionally. On her mobile, he recalled belatedly. Ten years ago Lorna would have been seventeen, she could have been a pupil at the senior school during

Janice Meek's first year as head of the juniors. 'Would it be possible for you to check your records and see if Lorna attended the senior school? She would have been seventeen when you arrived.'

Out of kindness she arranged for it to be done although she suspected it was a waste of time. The girl, whoever she was, had cruelly set out to deceive him. However, had this Lorna been a pupil and gone on to further education there would be a record of the college or university. Mr Pearce might have more luck there. They drank coffee while the secretary went over to the senior school to check the records. She drew a blank.

'I'm so sorry,' Mrs Meek said. 'The only other thing I can suggest is that you contact the people who deal with the register of teachers. If she did qualify she'll be on the list.'

He wrote down the details and stood up to leave. The woman was busy, she had looked at her watch twice during the last few minutes. 'Thank you for your time, I appreciate it,' he said, hoping the bitter disappointment didn't show too much. It was as if Lorna Daniels had never existed.

Dave Johnson was discharged from hospital at lunchtime on Thursday. He was in considerable pain and would need to rest for a while but he would make a full recovery. In a week's time his GP would remove the stitches. Before that he was expecting another visit from the police. The detective who had sat by his hospital bed had been far from satisfied with his story. Dave would deal with that problem when the time came.

Very carefully he levered himself from the taxi that dropped him outside the small terraced house whose front door opened straight on to the street. His wife had visited him briefly on Tuesday and Wednesday but hadn't bothered to come and collect him. She heard the diesel engine and came to the door. She would be off for her two until ten shift at the supermarket soon but she had time to get him something to eat and to settle him down. She was amazed they'd let him out so quickly but assumed this was due to a shortage of beds.

Dave was surprised when she took his arm and led him to a chair in the kitchen. He must look awful for her to be treating him so solicitously.

'What happened, Dave?' she asked as she plugged in the kettle and got out bread for sandwiches. 'The knife was yours, wasn't it? I can't imagine Dennis carrying one.'

He studied his wife's well-padded form and her slightly stringy hair. If she made a bit of effort she could still pass for good-looking. Despite the fact that they now led almost separate lives he could still tell her things he knew she would never repeat. Myra wasn't stupid, she knew he supplemented his unemployment benefit money with cash-in-hand jobs. After two consecutive redundancies from the building trade several months of depression had followed and he had long since given up hope of finding another full-time job.

'I was asked to do someone a favour, for cash, love. I don't know what came over Dennis. Even if he overheard the deal it was no skin off his nose. Admittedly he was out of his head but as soon as we were outside he grabbed the knife out of my pocket and that was that. I don't know how he even knew it was there. I'm not going to court, though, I won't stitch him up.'

Or yourself, she thought. 'Will you do this favour, this thing you were asked?'

'Yes.' He smiled. He would gain in two ways. He had never been caught in his shady dealings and minor criminal career: he was painstakingly careful and only did jobs he knew could be done successfully, and never at regular intervals, that was always a giveaway. This one would be a piece of cake when he was well enough to do it.

Myra handed him a corned beef and mustard sandwich, his favourite. 'Will you be all right while I'm at work?'

'Yes, I'll lie on the sofa and watch a bit of

TV. That's all I'm fit for at the moment.'

'Want me to leave you something to eat for later?'

'No, I'll phone for a takeaway.' He grinned. 'I can make it to the door and back.'

She sat and drank tea with him then went upstairs to get ready for work.

On Thursday morning, recalling what Peter Bennett had told him about the Jones family the previous night, Ian telephoned the station. He asked for someone to find out their address and to ring him back. 'I'll be in about eleven, I'm going to pay them a visit,' he told Alan Campbell when he came back to him with the information. He then drove towards Little Endesley to the address he had been given.

The sky was now overcast, and the humidity was rising. There would be a much-needed storm before long.

The small council estate was typical of any that could be found throughout the country. The houses were uniform and had the same-sized gardens but there the similarities ended. Some had neat lawns, flowerbeds and hanging baskets, others nothing more than a dreary concrete frontage, and one or two had the usual assortment of accumulated rubbish on the patchy grass. Ian was surprised that single parent Mrs Jones had time to attend to hanging baskets and the well-kept garden.

Inside a radio was playing loudly but the occupant heard the bell when it rang because she came to the door immediately. 'Mrs Jones?' He showed her his identity.

'You'd better come in,' she said with resignation.

He followed her slim form to the clean and tidy kitchen where she lowered the volume on the radio. For a woman with no husband and four sons she had worn well. She was in the middle of making some sort of stew. 'For my father,' she explained. 'He's getting on and he lives on his own. I take it you've come about one of the boys?'

'I'd like to ask them a few questions, if I may. Are any of them in?'

'All of them. Two are in bed, the other two are watching a video.'

He had heard what he thought was a television when they had passed a closed door in the narrow entrance hall. 'May I speak to them?'

She nodded. 'In here. I'll get the others up.'

The two boys in the living-room were about ten and thirteen. They looked shocked when their mother switched off the TV without ceremony. 'Just answer the Chief Inspector's questions,' she told them.

'Mrs Jones, they're minors, I need you to stay, please.'

'All right. Billy, you go and get Charlie and Joe up and tell them to make it quick. This is Steven,' she added, referring to the older boy.

'Steven, do you know anything about the fire that was started on Monday night when a garage was burnt down?'

He looked at his mother with a panic-stricken face.

'I'm not suggesting you were responsible, I only want to know if you'd heard anything about it.'

He shook his head. 'I don't know nothing.'

Ian took the double negative to mean no. 'You've been in trouble before, haven't you?'

'Not me, two of my brothers.'

'That's right,' Mrs Jones confirmed. 'Charlie and Joe. I've never understood what makes them do it. Joe's left school now and takes work when he can find it. I'm hoping he'll straighten out if he gets a permanent job. The other three have broken up a few days early because they're building more classrooms at the school and they couldn't fit the whole job into the summer holidays.'

Billy must be older than he looked if he went to the same school as his brothers.

The two older boys were tousled from bed. All four denied any knowledge of the fire at Phillip Hardy's place, other than they had heard it had taken place. 'Who'd want to set an empty garage alight?' Joe asked.

'Who'd be stupid enough to want to set anything alight?' Ian asked by way of reply, causing the first-born son to blush. 'If you do hear anything please ring us at Rickenham Green.' Wasted words, they wouldn't, of course, but for some reason he believed they were telling the truth about the fire. At least it had been worth a try. And the boys might be less inclined to pyromania now that they had received a personal visit from a detective chief inspector. He could but hope.

Audrey Field received the first telephone call during the early hours of Wednesday morning. Anna had insisted she had an extension beside her bed. Groggy with sleep she reached out, put on the bedside light and lifted the receiver hoping it wasn't bad news, praying that Robbie hadn't done anything stupid. There was no one there. She cursed at the click as the line was disconnected followed only by the dialling tone – a wrong number, a drunk, someone playing a joke, maybe – and hoped she'd be able to get back to sleep.

She thought no more about it until the same thing happened on Thursday. For the second time she tapped out 1471 but the caller had again withheld their number. It was then that she began to worry. She would mention it to Anna when she next saw her.

Could this be the third thing, Anna wondered as they sat drinking tea in Audrey's cottage. The storm had broken after lunch and rain was washing down the windows. 'If it happens again we'll contact the telephone people and see if they can do anything about it.' The police wouldn't be interested, not unless the calls were threatening or abusive, and Audrey's caller hadn't spoken. Perhaps it was a genuine mistake or there was a fault on the line. Such things did happen but she couldn't bear to see her mother so upset.

At least I don't have to go to work, I can spend my time with her when necessary, Anna thought. Initially she had missed her job in the London art gallery where she had met John but once she was pregnant and they had moved to Little Endesley more and more things had filled her time. First baby Robbie, then she had helped at the nursery school as a volunteer, and over the years she had gradually became involved in the various affairs of the village. When John died the house had been paid for and his pension schemes and insurance policies more than covered all her expenses. He had been a methodical man.

His sudden death had shocked her but at least she had been with him when he died and she had had the support of her friends and family. And now she had Phillip whom she loved although not in quite the same way. 'Come over for dinner tonight, Mum. Phillip will drop you back if you don't want to stay the night.' Anna's house was large but Audrey refused to move in, she insisted on retaining her independence.

'I'd like that. Have you heard anything from Robbie?'

'Yes, he's spoken to the solicitors who dealt with the sale of the house where Lorna was supposed to be living. They're going to try to contact the previous owner who is now in the States. And he went to the school this morning but no one had heard of her there. It seems she had no intention of going through with the marriage. I can't imagine what she was playing at but I can't think of anything more cruel than what she's done to him.'

'I just hope he gets over it and that it doesn't put him off women for ever.'

'He has youth on his side.' Anna paused. 'I really don't want him to find her.'

'Don't you? I think he'd feel easier if he knew the truth. He at least deserves an explanation.'

'Maybe. Look, I must go, Mum. I've got some shopping to do and I need to hand in the petition for the pelican crossing in the village. Come up this evening whenever you're ready.'

'Thank you, darling. I'll see you later.' She

walked to the door with her daughter, her face pale from lack of sleep. They had always been a happy, lucky family, possibly too lucky because lately things had started to go very wrong.

Anna put up her umbrella and walked to her car, turning once to wave.

Detective Inspector John Short was sent to speak to Dave Johnson to see if he could get any sense out of him.

Johnson hobbled to the door on Friday morning trying to look worse than he felt and therefore gain some sympathy. Myra was on the eight until two shift and need not know of this visit. 'Come in off the street,' he said, aware of the curious stare of a neighbour and the fact that it was raining again.

Short shook raindrops off his mac and followed him to the front room. The television was on and there was a mug and an ashtray beside an armchair. He had obviously not interrupted anything important. The small room was plainly decorated but clean and tidy. He was surprised to notice books on a shelf.

'It's about Tuesday, I suppose,' Johnson said before any introductions had been made. 'I can't tell you any more than what I told the other bloke.'

That's what they all say, Short thought as

he followed Johnson's lead and sat down. 'We hoped your memory might have improved with time.'

'Nothing wrong with my memory when I haven't had a skinful. If you ask me it was an accident.'

'An accident?' Short tugged at his moustache and listened to the rain driving against the window. He was likely to get more sense out of those pattering sounds than the ones coming from Johnson's mouth.

But he seemed to come to a decision. 'See, it was my knife. I reckon Dennis realized how pissed I was and tried to take it off me in case I did something stupid. That's how it was. These things happen.'

'Do you usually carry a knife?'

'No. I'd got it with me because I was doing a few jobs for an old lady I know.'

How touching. The villain with a heart of gold. Except he's got no record, Short remembered. 'And the lady's name and address, please?'

Johnson supplied them without hesitation. He was probably telling the truth, about that if nothing else.

'Anyway, I'm on the mend. No harm done, as they say. Best to leave it there, don't you think?'

Why? Short wondered. And why couldn't Dennis Suitor recall what had provoked him? Because something must have done.

People didn't pull a knife for nothing. But he saw he was wasting his time. Johnson was going to stick to that story. He would be an obstructive witness. Suitor had only admitted what he had done because he had been told there were witnesses. If Johnson swore it was an accident and there were no hard feelings there was little they could do.

He went back out into the rain wondering what it was that one or both men had to hide.

It was almost lunchtime – at least, near enough for John Short. He stopped to buy a burger and ate it whilst illegally parked on double yellow lines. The smell of onions filled the car and the windows misted over. The Chief wouldn't be thrilled with the outcome of his conversation but there wasn't much he could do about that. Had Brenda questioned Johnson there might have been a different outcome. She had that effect on men, an ability to make them say more than they needed just for the pleasure of looking at her. But the lovely Brenda would not be back with them until Monday.

They could bring their own charges against Suitor, Ian was perfectly aware of that, but if, as Short reported, Johnson was prepared to swear it was an accident and Suitor had no recollection of the events of Tuesday morning then it would be a waste of time.

Johnson's story about the old lady had checked out. She was a friend of Myra Johnson's mother. 'We can't even do him for carrying an offensive weapon,' Short said, interrupting Ian's pessimistic thoughts.

'Who?' The elusive woman in the case had been on his mind. Why would someone such as had been described by Tony Peak, the landlord, have been in the Black Horse, alone, in the first place?

'Johnson. It was his knife. He'd been using it on a job before he called in for a drink on his way home. Some drink, mind you, if it lasted all night.'

'I'll have a word with the Super but I imagine he won't want to run with this. Anything new on the fire?'

'No. I can't see that progressing any further either.'

Only when Short had left the office did Ian realize that he had managed to relay his information without the use of a single cliché. It was almost a matter for cele-bration, except for the fact that the smell of greasy food which clung to Short's clothes still lingered in the room.

Chapter Eight

The downpour continued the whole of Friday but petered out during the early hours of the morning. Rain had been much needed and Ian woke to a sunny but fresher Saturday. He sat in the garden surrounded by flowers which no longer drooped. Droplets of moisture sparkled on the longer blades of grass and the leaves of the runner beans where they wound their way around their canes. He picked up his mug of coffee and opened the weekly edition of the *Rickenham Herald* which came out on Fridays but which he had not yet had a chance to read. The fire at Hardy's place and the stabbing outside the Black Horse were both mentioned, the latter featuring on the front page, but the articles contained no more than the information the police press officer had given to the reporter. In the case of the fire, witnesses were asked to come forward but no one yet had rung the number printed beneath the article. Ian doubted if anyone ever would.

'I'm going into town. Is there anything you want?' Moira asked as she appeared at his side.

'No. Not unless we're out of beer.'

'How typical. But no, we're not. I won't be very long.' She kissed the top of his head and squealed when he slapped her jeans-clad behind. 'I wish you wouldn't do that. You don't know your own strength sometimes.'

Ian grinned. 'Kiss it better, shall I?'

'Not right now, thank you. And don't forget Mum's coming today.'

'I won't.' Ian liked Philippa and always enjoyed her company although it felt odd to be nearer his mother-in-law's age than that of his wife. Because Philippa would be staying for several nights Moira had taken the week off. At the end of September, when the children would be back at their schools and things would be generally quieter, he and Moira were going away for a fortnight. As yet they didn't know where. Ian hoped to persuade Moira against going abroad. He hated foreign travel. Perhaps the West Country might appeal. I'll get Philippa on my side, she prefers to stay in England, he thought as he got up to make another drink. The weekend lay ahead. He would simply relax and go along with whatever his two favourite women decided they wanted to do.

It was the weather that made up their minds. Taking advantage of the continuing warmth they ate in the garden of a country pub on Saturday evening and took a trip to the coast on Sunday. Ian noted with sadness that Philippa had slowed down a little since last he'd seen her and the heat bothered her more than it used to. Otherwise she was her usual elegant and entertaining self with plenty of gossip about her many friends. Tactfully, Ian kept off the subject of work.

On Monday morning he left Moira and Philippa planning how they would spend the day. Arriving at the station he saw Brenda getting out of her car. In the general office she was greeted with much ribaldry and referred to as Sarge far more often than was necessary. But they all knew she deserved her promotion.

'Did you good,' John Short said.

'What did?'

'The break.' He leered. 'What did you think I meant?'

'Knowing you, anything.' But she felt good. The week in Jersey had been wonderful but it was over too quickly.

Short grinned. He liked and respected Brenda but she was still a woman and therefore fair game.

Brenda was too busy catching up with the events of the week to notice him studying her slim, brown legs beneath the desk. Flinging back her long chestnut hair she began tapping away at her computer. 'What's all this about a missing woman? The name Pearce rings a bell.'

'It's a common enough name. It was me he spoke to.' Greg Grant walked across the general office and stood behind Brenda's chair.

'Mm, but the address, I know that, too.' She chewed the end of a biro. 'Yes, I remember now. Pearce was the name of that antiques expert. Paintings mostly, I believe. He was quite a local celebrity in his time. He travelled all over the world and appeared on TV now and then. I know he lived out at Little Endesley.'

'How do you know all this?' It was Short who asked.

'Because Andrew was talking about him a few weeks ago. He's got a painting he knows nothing about except it's been in the family for ever and he said that had John Pearce still been around he'd have asked him to take a look at it. They played golf together a couple of times.'

'Has he moved away?' Greg asked.

'No. He's dead. He died suddenly about five or six years ago from a heart attack. His son was just finishing at university, Andrew told me, but he didn't live to see him graduate.'

'And you reckon this Robert Pearce is his son?'

'Probably, if his mother lives at Little Endesley. And he sounds about the right age. What is it?' Both men were frowning as the same thought crossed their minds.

Short shook his head. 'The fire was out there, too. No, there can't be any connection. Besides, as you can see, this girl disappeared in London.'

Brenda, seated, looked up at the Inspector. He was no prettier for being viewed from below. 'Poor Pearce. Fancy being let down right at the very last minute.' Having had such a brilliant wedding herself she could imagine how devastating it must have been for him.

'Pearce's story was a bit strange but I checked locally and ran her through the computer in case there was something we ought to be looking into – and there's no mention of a Lorna Daniels living in our district or having a criminal record. I told Pearce to report it to his local police. Look lively, here's the Chief.'

Ian, who had not had a chance to speak to Brenda in the car park, had gone straight to his office to check for messages. He now welcomed her back and began the morning's briefing.

Brenda, trying to concentrate after a week of not having to think about anything other than where to eat or which place to visit, decided she would ask Andrew if he knew anything about John Pearce's son. Under the circumstances it was odd that he should have contacted the Rickenham Green police. When the briefing was over she mentioned the little she knew of the Pearces to Ian.

Robbie's patience was wearing thin but until the solicitor came back to him there was little he could do. He had been totally convinced that Lorna was a teacher. Everything she had told him about her training and job rang true but no one with that name was on the register of teachers within an area where she could feasibly have travelled to work each day. Now he was regretting not having any photographs of her because he realized she had probably been using a false name along with the other lies she had told him. He had a camera but rarely used it. Photography did not interest him and he wasn't much good at it. But not one photograph in a relationship which had lasted almost two years... Was that unusual? Had he ever tried to take any of her and she'd refused? He didn't know, but there were so many things he didn't know. For instance, what had Lorna been playing at? He had been so certain she had loved him.

There was another whole week of his leave left but he had nothing to do except wait. Perhaps he would go back to his mother's later in the week. With no breeze to stir the heat which was trapped between the buildings the temperature in London was unbearable but for the moment he wanted to be there in case Barbara Hughes telephoned with news.

On Wednesday morning, as he still dithered about what to do next, he discovered that the decision had been made for him. One telephone call altered everything for both Robbie Pearce and the police.

They had planned to go to Saxborough. Audrey wanted a new outfit to wear to a friend's Golden Wedding anniversary party, and Anna had said she would drive her there and treat her to lunch as well.

At 8.40 a.m. Anna picked up the phone to warn her mother she'd be late. The kitchen sink had sprung a leak and she needed to contact a plumber. No one would be able to come that day, she knew that much about plumbers, and it wasn't an emergency, she had placed a bowl beneath the U-bend to catch the drips, but the sooner she arranged for the job to be done, the better.

After letting the phone ring for what seemed a long time Anna tried again in case she had misdialled. There was still no answer. It was too late for Audrey to be in the bath or shower as she was expecting Anna at nine. Perhaps she was in the garden. Replacing the receiver she tried the next plumber on her list and was rewarded with a human voice rather than an answering machine and was promised that he would come the following afternoon. Anna thanked him and hurried out to the car.

Immediately she pulled up in the street outside the cottage she knew that something was wrong. The curtains were still drawn, upstairs and down. Fear making her mouth dry, she walked up the path and tried to unlock the front door with the spare key on her ring. It wouldn't open but Audrey would have shot the bolts before she went to bed.

Trembling, she made her way around the side of the house. The kitchen door was closed but unlocked. A pane of glass was missing. 'Mum?' But even before the word was out of her mouth she was rushing towards the chair in which Audrey sat, bound and gagged, her head lolling unnaturally to one side. 'Oh, no. Oh, God, no,' she whispered, swallowing the bile which rose in her throat as she clutched the back of the chair to steady herself.

Roughly, because she was shaking so much, she removed the gag from her mother's mouth and lifted her head. She knew, even as she rang for an ambulance and the police, that it was already too late.

'What the hell's going on out there?' Ian asked rhetorically as he fastened his seat-belt.

Inspector Short had gone on ahead. Ian was following with Brenda. Short was perfectly capable of dealing with things; it was an inspector's job to get things organized at the scene of a serious crime, especially murder. Except this wasn't technically a murder inquiry. However, once the uniformed officer who had first attended the scene had contacted CID and Sergeant Brenda Osborne had pointed out that the name Pearce seemed to be prominent lately, Ian decided he wanted to have a look for himself.

'The thing is, sir,' Brenda was saying as she pulled out into the main road, 'I spoke to Andrew and he said that he'd heard that Anna Pearce was seeing Phillip Hardy. Andrew doesn't know anything about the son except he is called Robbie. He's never met him.'

As Brenda drove he tried to piece it all together. Robbie Pearce's bride goes missing on her wedding day, Anna Pearce is seeing Phillip Hardy whose garage burns down and nearly sets fire to his house as well, and now Audrey Field, Anna's mother and Robert's grandmother, is the victim of a burglary which has gone wrong and left her dead in her own kitchen. The crime must have taken place sometime after dark as the constable who reported to them said that all the curtains had still been drawn when the daughter arrived.

They would now have to take Lorna Daniels' disappearance seriously. Something may have happened to her, too. Except Sergeant Grant had been told by Robbie Pearce that the bride did not live at the address where he claimed he had visited her on many occasions.

Anna Pearce was sitting on the bench in front of the house oblivious to the movements of the crime team and the stares of people in the village street. She was numb and so full of pain and grief she couldn't even cry. Beside her, far from impassive, sat a good-looking man in his early fifties. Short, who had met him before, introduced him as Phillip Hardy then took Ian and Brenda to one side out of Anna Pearce's hearing. 'SOCOs and photographers are here but there's no sign of the pathologist yet. It doesn't look like our man had any intention of killing her, there aren't any visible injuries, but she died anyway.

'The daughter's only been in the kitchen, she telephoned from there. Until our lot have finished we won't know if anything's missing.' He nodded in Anna's direction. 'She's not up to telling us yet anyway.'

'Does she need a doctor?' Ian was aware what a shock it would have been for her.

'She says not, sir.'

'Brenda, fill John in with your knowledge

of the family.'

She did so, although it didn't amount to much. Short whistled through his teeth. 'They're not having much luck between them at the moment. It can hardly all be coincidence, can it?'

As much as Ian didn't believe in coincidence it could still be the case here. There was nothing to link the fire and the burglary, and Lorna's disappearance may have simply been a last-minute change of heart. Coincidence, maybe, or as Short had suggested, bad luck. But Ian didn't believe in luck, good or bad, either.

The sun was moving higher in the sky, shining directly on them where they stood. Ian was grateful for the short-sleeved shirt and lightweight trousers he was wearing. The thickness of his hair protected his head. Scruffy Short, however, was living up to his name and was over-dressed in a brown, rumpled suit and suede shoes. Beads of sweat stood out between the strands of dark hair stretched across his bald pate but he didn't show any other signs of noticing the heat. Brenda, as always, looked cool and clean in a yellow summer dress and sandals. Her gleaming hair was held back at the nape of her neck with a tortoiseshell slide.

There was now a small crowd of people on the pavement beyond the low, stone wall. They stared at the figures in the garden with open curiosity. Ian gestured for one of the PCs who had arrived at the house in response to Anna's call to disband them. With many backward glances they moved off reluctantly.

The pathologist finally arrived and was taken around the side of the cottage to the kitchen entrance everyone had used to avoid contaminating evidence elsewhere in the house. He was not there long. 'All the signs point to heart failure,' he said to Ian before he left. 'No other injuries apart from slight bruising to the upper arms and some redness where the ropes bound her wrists. They were probably caused by her struggling to try to free herself rather than anything that was done to her. She's been dead for at least six or seven hours, possibly longer. Well, that's it, I'm afraid. I'll be off now.'

Ian nodded and thanked him. He knew it was impossible to give a time of death with any accuracy. As the curtains were drawn and Audrey Field was wearing a nightdress a fool could have worked out that whoever broke in and tied her up had done it sometime after dark and before daylight. And daylight came early now.

'I've rung for the van, it's on its way. You know where to reach me if you've any queries.' The pathologist walked swiftly back to his car, his bag in his hand.

'Not the most forthcoming of men,' Short commented as he tugged at his moustache.

'Jackson? No, never has been. I don't suppose there's much he can say in this instance.' And Ian preferred it that way. Some pathologists he had encountered imagined themselves as detectives.

Another wait followed as the scene-of-crime team went over the house. Ian sent the young and shaken PC down to the mini-supermarket to buy some cans of cold drinks. Anna Pearce looked desperately in need of something and they couldn't get to the kitchen to make tea. When the PC returned and the drinks were handed round Ian went across to where Anna and Phillip were sitting. He wanted to speak to her but he also wanted to try to block her view of the mortuary van which was just pulling up in the road. 'Mrs Pearce? I'm Chief Inspector Roper. There isn't much one can say in these circumstances but I'm very sorry about what's happened to your mother.'

She looked up and blinked. Her expression was blank, her face pale beneath her tan. 'Would it have been quick? Did she suffer?' she asked, as did almost everyone who was connected with an unexpected death.

'I doubt it, certainly not for long.' Ian answered with as much honesty as possible. Heart failure had been the cause of his father's death and was one of the reasons

Moira kept a careful eye on his diet and managed to talk him out of smoking every so often, although his good intentions never lasted long. According to his mother, who had been in the same room at the time, Henry Roper had said 'Good heavens, Amy,' as he put a hand to his chest and fell to the floor. 'It was over in seconds, Ian,' she'd told him. A year later she had died herself. 'This is Sergeant Gibb ... Osborne.' Ian corrected himself knowing he had better get used to the name quickly. 'If you feel up to it she's going to ask you some questions, but if you'd rather wait until later just say so.'

Anna nodded. 'Yes, now's fine. I just hope I can be of help.'

Phillip stood to allow room for Brenda to sit on the bench. 'Am I in the way?' he asked as he followed Ian across the small patch of lawn bordered by flowerbeds in which bees flew to and fro. The scent of lavender was almost overpowering as their legs brushed the drying flowers.

'No. Mrs Pearce will need you when we've gone. But don't go into the house until we say so.' As he spoke the men from the mortuary came around the side of the house bearing a stretcher upon which Audrey Field lay wrapped in a body-bag. There was no way in which they could remove her without being seen by her daughter and anyone who happened to be passing in the street. Fortunately the row of shops was further down the road, which curved slightly, so there were few spectators.

Anna caught her breath and put her hand to her mouth as her mother was taken away but still she didn't cry. She wished Robbie was there with her but at least he was on his way. Immediately after she had rung the emergency services she had spoken to Phillip then to Robbie. Both had said they would come right away. Her words had been gabbled, she wasn't sure how much of what she'd said Robbie had understood.

'Tell me what happened this morning, Anna. Take your time but try and recall exactly what you did.' Anna Pearce's actions were not important unless she had tampered with the crime scene. What Brenda was hoping to achieve by asking this question was for Anna to be able to get her thoughts in order in case there was something she could recall which would help them solve the case. For instance, had Mrs Field ever mentioned to anyone that she possessed anything valuable?

Anna inhaled deeply. 'All right. I was running late. I tried to phone Mum but I couldn't get any answer. I wasn't particularly worried, if she was in the garden she wouldn't have heard the phone, you see. She's a little bit deaf but she won't admit it.'

She paused, feeling guilty that she had not been more worried, that she'd rung a plumber instead of rushing to the cottage. But a few minutes wouldn't have made any difference, she knew that really. 'I'd told her I'd be here by nine. It was about ten or quarter past when I finally got here. She's an early riser but the curtains were still drawn. That's how I knew ... how I knew something awful had happened.' She explained how she'd tried to get in with the spare key she insisted she kept for emergencies and that the glass had been broken in the back door. 'That's when I saw her. I think I knew right away but part of me hoped I wasn't too late. I untied the gag but she wasn't breathing. Then I rang you.'

'Anna, did you touch anything?'

'Yes, the door and the phone and the chair, I think, but I really don't know about anything else. I know I just stood there, looking at her until the police arrived.'

The PCs had gone around the back and found Anna and her mother and everything just as she had described it. 'We'll need you to have a look around later to see if you can tell us if anything's missing.'

'Yes, of course.'

Brenda studied the woman's profile. Even in grief she was attractive. Good bones and a clear complexion but no effort had been made to disguise the silvery hairs amongst the natural blonde ones. Her figure was good with barely a hint of thickening around the waist and hips. The plain linen dress was simple and tasteful and probably expensive. The blue matched her eyes. Her shoes and bag were of a slightly darker blue. Brenda wished she could afford accessories to match every outfit. Her brown leather sandals went with most of her summer clothes.

The scene-of-crime team finished just as the detectives waiting outside were really beginning to feel the effects of the sun which was now almost directly overhead. In the distance a heat haze shimmered over the surface of the road. Brenda glanced at the Chief, who nodded. Anna Pearce was free to check if anything had been taken.

'I can't understand any of this,' Phillip Hardy said to Ian whilst Anna was recounting the earlier events of the morning to Brenda. He looked haggard and at the end of his tether.

'Tell us about Anna's son,' Ian said.

'You surely can't think he had anything to do with this? He adored his grandmother.'

'I meant about the abortive wedding.' Ian evaded the question. For the moment everyone was a suspect. Audrey Fields might have a will leaving everything to her daughter, her only child, a daughter who might need the money urgently. Maybe she was aware her mother had heart problems and had terrified her in such a way as to make it seem as if there had been an intruder. Her fingerprints would naturally be all over the house. The same scenario might also be applied to the grandson. However, unless money was not the motive, Hardy was in the clear. His financial standing had been checked after the fire and what they had learned had caused a few whistles and many moans of envy. 'I certainly wouldn't continue working if I was in his shoes,' Short had said predictably.

'He'd known Lorna for nearly a year when he asked her to marry him. Anna had known for ages that he was serious about her, even before we met her. She said she could tell by the way he spoke of her.

'Anyway, she started to come down to Mulberry Cottage with Robbie. That's where Anna lives, by the way, and until he went away to university it was where Robbie had spent the whole of his life. We all got on well with Lorna, more than got on with, she became part of the family. She'd go over and see Audrey, too. We grew to love her. There was something about her, a sort of vulnerability underneath her great sense of fun. She was a teacher.' He shrugged. 'Well, that's what she told us. Robbie's been doing some checking and it seems she doesn't appear on the register. Anyway, she always seemed eager to please Anna and Audrey, and I was extremely flattered when she asked me to give her away.'

'Why you?' It seemed a little unconventional for the lover of the bridegroom's mother to take the bride down the aisle.

'There was no one else. Her mother was a single parent and Lorna never knew who her father was. The mother died in a road accident some years ago. She didn't have any other family and she wanted an older man to give her away rather than a male friend her own age.

'I just don't understand it, she seemed so happy making all the arrangements and booking the honeymoon. I still find it hard to believe it's happened. And now this.'

Ian wanted to know a bit more about the wedding. 'What happened on the actual day, at the church?'

Phillip explained how he had gone to the house only to learn that new people had moved in and they'd never heard of Lorna Daniels. That was as much as he could tell him. 'Going into that church to let them all know was one of the hardest things I've ever had to do.'

'And the guests?'

'What about them?'

'How many were there from Lorna's side?'

'About half a dozen. It wasn't a big do. Well, it wasn't a do at all in the end. We, the family, that is, came straight back down here. Anna insisted that the guests go to the hotel where the reception was to have been held. Everything would have been wasted otherwise.'

'Would you know how we can contact Lorna's guests?'

'No, but Anna probably would. She sent out the invitations. Being a bride without a mother or father Lorna was only too pleased for Anna to take over the role. You're taking her disappearance seriously, aren't you?'

'We have to now.'

'If you find her it might make Robbie feel better but it isn't going to help Anna. She's going to miss Audrey dreadfully.' He glanced towards the cottage as if he wanted to be inside with Anna. 'At least Robbie's on his way, she'll need him now, possibly more than she needs me.'

So the son was arriving soon. Ian and Short exchanged a glance. It would save contacting the Met. Robert Pearce would have to be interviewed, far better that it was on their own doorstep.

Anna and Brenda came out through the front door. 'We have a list, sir, although Anna isn't sure if it's complete. The few things that're missing are all small and could easily have been carried by one person.'

Ian took the list. Some silver, the value unknown to Anna, a couple of figurines, a

Staffordshire wall plate and a few bits of jewellery. Things that could easily be fenced.

'Not the usual stuff,' Short commented, reading over Ian's shoulder. He was referring to electronic goods which could be flogged for a couple of notes in the pub. But Audrey Field had been in her seventies: anyone who knew that would have guessed it was unlikely she owned a computer or any of the other modern technology considered essential by some. 'Are we going in now?'

'Yes. Sergeant Osborne, would you take Mrs Pearce home and stay with her until her son arrives?' Hardy could have done so, Ian had actually asked him to stay for that reason, but he now thought that Anna might be more willing to talk to a female, one who was a stranger. She might just remember something that would throw light on to what was happening to her family.

'Will you be all right, Anna?'

'Yes. You go back to work, Phillip. Come up when you've finished. Robbie should be here soon and Brenda will be with me until then.'

'What about your car?'

'I'll pick it up another time.' Shock was setting in. Despite the heat of the day Anna began to shiver and her legs felt as though they'd give way any minute. She was not fit

to drive even the few hundred yards to
Mulberry Cottage. Gratefully she slid into
the passenger seat beside Brenda Osborne.

Chapter Nine

Dave Johnson had carried out the favour that had been asked of him even before he'd had his stitches removed, although favour was hardly the word. There had been no danger involved, nor had he taken any risks, but there had been a timetable to adhere to. He'd been paid for his efforts; paid in part, the rest was still to come. He suspected getting it might turn out to be a problem.

The job had been a pushover and it had all gone more smoothly than he could have hoped. He had already received fifty pounds in advance. There was another fifty to follow if the job was done by a certain date, which it was, and, of course, there were the other perks. He'd had no choice but to take the promise of the second payment on trust. Too late he realized that he had no way of contacting his temporary employer and that he'd probably been taken for a ride. Still, fifty notes and what else he'd got out of it wasn't bad for an hour's work. And he wasn't going to draw attention to himself by trying to get the rest of the money should he be let down.

At twelve fifteen on the pre-arranged date

he told Myra, who had a day off, that he wouldn't be long then he walked down to the Black Horse where he was welcomed back warmly by those who hadn't seen him since the incident with Dennis Suitor. 'It was an accident,' Dave told them. 'Sodding idiot thought I might do some damage with the knife and tried to take it off me.' This was the story he would continue to repeat to anyone who asked. He knew that Dennis had been released because he had now made a statement to the police to the effect that the stabbing was an accident. There was little the police could do. If they changed their minds and brought their own charges he would go into the witness box and swear to the very same thing.

He needed to speak to Dennis, to make sure he didn't recall the reason why the knife had ended up in his hand and Dave had ended up in hospital. He had never known Dennis to drink as much as he'd done during that long night so it was doubtful if he would ever recall what had happened. Dave knew what alcohol could do to the memory but he also knew why Dennis had pulled the knife.

The appointed time for the meeting came and went. No one turned up. Dave waited another hour then, metaphorically, shrugged his shoulders and went home to Myra bearing half a bottle of vodka as a peace offering because he was far later than he had anticipated.

The cottage was typical of one lived in by a member of the older generation. The small but essential comforts of life that were left lying around were evidence of the inhabitant's age. A thick raincoat and hat hung on the back of the kitchen door, a pair of slippers stood to one side of it. Not the slippers Audrey had been wearing, they were for the bedroom and bathroom, less practical than the ones she wore about the house. In the sitting-room a rug was folded over the arm of a chair and a small table beside it held reading glasses, a lamp and a cork mat upon which to place hot drinks. There was knitting in a carpet-bag beside the chair.

Short had gone back to the station to set up the paperwork. Ian and Brenda were joined by Alan Campbell as they went through each room systematically. I don't know why we're doing this, Ian thought. Audrey Field was not a murder victim although the charge would undoubtedly be manslaughter. But there just might be something to point them in the right direction; a signed threatening letter would make his day. He shook his head. There was no point in hoping for the impossible.

The kitchen contained the usual appliances

but few modern gadgets. There was fresh food in the fridge, bread in the bin and a bowl of fruit on the worktop. They could smell the ripening peaches. The drawers and cupboards revealed no secrets. They held tinned and packet food, cutlery and an assortment of junk. There was a handknitted cosy for the chipped blue pot.

Audrey's papers were kept in a small bureau in the corner of the sitting-room. There weren't many and they were all on a prong in date order. She obviously owned the cottage as the deeds were there in a folder, but although she had some small investments there was nothing to suggest she was wealthy. It seemed another theory was out of the window. But Ian could not believe that this was the work of the average burglar. Surely, if disturbed he would have run off or, seeing his victim was elderly, simply pushed her to the ground. Why risk all those minutes it would have taken to tie her to the chair?

'The rope,' he said. 'We didn't ask Anna Pearce if it belonged to her mother.'

'She might not know,' Alan replied.

'No, but it would have to have been handy. Whoever was here wouldn't have started searching cupboards and drawers while Mrs Pearce looked on.'

'He might've brought it with him, sir.'

'Exactly. In which case, why?'

It was a question they thought about as they continued their search upstairs. There were two bedrooms. The larger one at the front was pretty and feminine and was where Audrey had slept. The bed was unmade. Beside it, on a small table, lay a pair of glasses, a mug which had contained tea and a paperback book. A small alarm clock ticked quietly. Over the back of a chair hung a cotton skirt and blouse, presumably the clothes she had worn the day before.

There were lavender bags amongst her clothes. Ian guessed that she made them herself from the plants which grew in the garden. Face powder filled a glass bowl on the dressing-table. Its faint flowery scent hung in the air. Nothing appeared to have been disturbed. There were no clothes on the floor, no drawers hanging open and nothing overturned. Something had happened here, something that was meant to look like breaking and entering but wasn't. Why only take small things from surfaces? Why leave the box of jewellery which lay open on the dressing-table? Something was wrong but Ian had no idea what it was.

Mid-afternoon they gave up and went back to the station.

John Short was tapping away at his computer using two fingers but making progress just as quickly as those who could work a keyboard using them all. He grunted.

Paperwork was consuming more and more time and discouraging officers from making an arrest. He knew it could take up to five hours to complete it properly, the length of time disproportionate to that spent detecting. 'Find anything?' he asked without looking up.

'No, nothing we didn't expect to find,' Ian replied.

'Brenda's back. The son's now returned to the bosom of what's left of his family.'

Ian picked up the telephone. If Robert Pearce had arrived he would go and see him immediately.

'Yes, of course he's prepared to speak to you any time you like,' Anna said in a voice which sounded nearly normal.

'Thank you. We'll be there in approximately twenty minutes.' Ian hung up. 'Eddie, if you're not busy you can come with me.'

They left the building and walked to where Ian's car was parked in one of the few allocated spaces at the back of the station. Most people had to use the underground car park. The car was uncomfortably hot even though he had parked it with the windscreen facing the wall and left the sunroof open a fraction.

'You're off tomorrow, aren't you, Eddie?'

'Yes, sir. It's my wife's cousin's wedding. They couldn't get a Saturday in July or August.'

Ian reversed out of his space and pointed the car towards the exit and the main road. It was all weddings lately, although there hadn't been one for Robbie Pearce. 'Exactly how many people are there in your combined families?' he asked as they waited at the traffic lights at the end of the road.

'About three hundred at the last count, I believe.'

Ian glanced at the detective constable seated beside him. Eddie was grinning but it might not have been a joke. In profile he was better looking than face on. Ian agreed with Moira that he had a pleasant face which reflected his nature. Eddie Roberts was kind and gentle and reliable but he was also firm and quietly determined. This showed in his work and the good behaviour of his children whom Ian had met on two occasions.

The roads were relatively quiet for four o'clock in the afternoon because there was no school traffic and no one wanted to be sitting in a car if they could be enjoying a summer afternoon out of doors. The village of Little Endesley was almost deserted.

Mulberry Cottage was not what they had expected. Ian had imagined it would be similar to Audrey Field's place. They turned into the drive which had the name of the house on the gate and pulled up on the wide sweep of gravel in front of the house. The large property was set in its own grounds.

The leaded window panes stood open, upstairs and down. They were the genuine article, not double-glazed reproductions. Ian wondered what the place would sell for. Phillip Hardy would know. He or his father had probably sold it to the Pearces in the first place. 'We'll take this gently.'

'Of course.' Eddie knew that the Chief did not wish to make Robbie Pearce feel threatened so soon after the bereavement.

'Come in, Chief Inspector,' Anna Pearce said when she had been introduced to DC Roberts. Ian was surprised she'd remembered his rank considering the state of shock she'd been in when he'd seen her that morning.

Ahead was a sweeping staircase with ornate banisters. They followed her past it, down the wide hallway, to the back of the house. The tall glass doors of the sitting-room stood open framing a well-maintained garden. From what he could see of the place Ian was sure Anna Pearce had no reason to wish her mother dead for lack of money. All was beautifully decorated and none of the furniture was shabby.

'This is my son, Robbie.'

'Hello.' He crossed the room from where he had been standing by the fireplace and extended his hand. It shook a little but his grip was firm.

Ian made the introductions again. There

was little resemblance between the mother and the son. Robbie's hair was dark and springy, his eyes were brown and he was more solidly built. Ian now vaguely recalled the father but only from press photographs and television appearances. He glanced at the mantelpiece. There was a framed photograph of the three of them taken when Robbie was in his teens. There was no question concerning his parentage. John Pearce had produced a child in his own image.

'Please sit down. Would you like some tea?'

'Thank you, Mrs Pearce, if it's no trouble.' It would give them a few minutes to sum up Robbie Pearce, and Anna, pale and shaking, seemed restless, as if she needed something to keep herself occupied. 'I'm very sorry about your grandmother,' Ian said once Anna had left the room. 'We'll do everything we can to find the intruder.' Oft-repeated words but Ian knew people took comfort from them.

'Yes, I know you will.' Robbie looked down at his hands which rested in his lap. 'Oh, God. I'm sorry.' He sniffed and wiped his eyes on his bare arm. 'I feel such a fool.'

Ian and Eddie waited. There was no shame in crying for the loss of someone you'd loved, someone you had known all your life.

'What a bloody awful summer this has been. I'm okay now. Please, ask your questions.'

Ian nodded at Eddie. He was closer in age to Robbie and might gain a quicker rapport.

'We're here on two counts. Firstly on your grandmother's behalf. As far your mother's concerned nothing much was taken but we wondered if you could think of a reason for anyone choosing Mrs Field's house as a target.'

'No. She didn't have a lot. Grandad left her enough to get by on and she owns ... owned the cottage, but that's about it. I don't think her savings amount to much and there weren't any real valuables. She didn't go in for collecting things, she didn't like clutter... Two reasons, you said?'

'Yes. We now feel we ought to try to locate Lorna Daniels.'

'You do?'

Both Ian and Eddie noticed his reaction. For a split second his face was animated and there was hope in his eyes. 'Yes. So what we'd like you to do is to tell us as much as you can about her.' Ian took over the interview just as Anna came in with a tray of tea. She poured and handed round cups then sat down.

Eddie made notes as Robbie began to speak. Ian watched the young man's body language. It was plain from that and the way in which his voice changed at certain points that he had loved the girl and was now hurting very badly from what she had done to him. Losing both Lorna and his grandmother in less than two weeks must be very hard to cope with.

'We'll follow up on everything you've told us,' Ian said as he placed his cup and saucer on the tray. He could certainly chase the solicitor, who might feel she had more important things to deal with than making a telephone call on behalf of Robbie Pearce. 'Mrs Pearce, I need to ask you this, do you know if your mother kept any rope in the house?'

Anna shook her head. Her hair fell forward. She brushed it back to reveal a face which reflected her grief. 'No. What would she need it for? There might be some in the shed but I doubt it.'

'I see. And the strip of material that was used as a gag, did you recognize that?'

Anna thought about it. 'No, I didn't. I mean, I didn't think at the time, I was more concerned with, well, you know.'

'There's one more thing,' Ian added as he stood. 'Do you still have the wedding guest list?'

'I'm not sure, but I think so.' She frowned. Her thoughts were with Audrey, they should be concentrating on her not the girl who had so badly deceived Robbie, deceived them all in fact. Then she felt ashamed. Robbie was suffering doubly. He should have been enjoying his honeymoon now. 'I'll go and look.' She left the room, walking slowly as if it was an effort, but there was still no sign that she had cried since her early morning discovery. That would come later, when the finality of it had sunk in properly.

'Why are you looking for her? You don't think she robbed Grandma, do you?' Robbie turned to Ian. His face was drawn and he looked ill as if he hadn't been sleeping properly.

'It's hard to know what to think at the moment but too many unpleasant things are happening to your family.'

'You said it. And there was the fire, too.' Anna had told him about it during a telephone conversation.

'You say you met Lorna at an art exhibition. Could she have known you'd be there?'

'No, definitely not. An invitation came to the flat. It was addressed to my father, he used to live there, you see. Anyway, I decided to go. Dad had thought highly of the artist.'

'Who sent the invitation?'

'Romano himself. The artist,' he added, seeing Ian's puzzled expression. 'The galleries hardly do anything for their

124

extortionate commission these days. Romano lives in Italy, he obviously hadn't heard about Dad.'

So it was a chance meeting. Lorna Daniels hadn't set him up from the beginning. So what had happened to make her lie about where she lived and to change her mind at the very last minute? From what Robbie had told them the Baxters' predecessor had been a fair-haired German woman in her fifties. The description could not possibly have fitted Miss Daniels. But was Robbie lying when he said he'd been to the house on many occasions? And if so, why? Naturally he was able to describe it, he had admitted that Vi Baxter had let him in.

Anna returned with a sheet of paper. 'There weren't many guests. About twenty-five and most of them were from our side.'

'Could you make a mark against those Lorna invited?'

Anna opened a drawer and got out a pen then handed the list to Ian.

'Thank you.' He ran his eye down the list but, as he had expected, none of the names meant anything to him. 'Had you met any of these people before?' he asked Robbie.

'No.' He shrugged. 'Neither of us are great socializers. We spent all our spare time together. I have the occasional drink with the blokes from work, but other than that, well, there was only Lorna. I'm a merchant banker, there's a lot of pressure with the job and Lorna had after-school activities with the children or meetings to attend so we were both often too tired to go out. At least, that's what she told me,' he added bitterly.

'Will you be here if we need to contact you again?'

Robbie looked at his mother. 'Stay as long as you like, you know you're always welcome. And right now I'd be more than glad of your company.'

'I'm due back at work on Monday. I don't suppose we'll be able to hold the funeral before then, even if we could arrange it in time.'

A death such as this would be reported to the Coroner's Officer but a second post-mortem would not be required as the cause of death would almost certainly turn out to be natural, even if it was brought about by events preceding it. The burial could therefore take place. 'There will have to be an inquest but you can go ahead and make whatever plans you choose.'

'I see.' And a post-mortem, Robbie realized but did not say because his mother might not be aware of the fact. 'I'll let you know if I return to London. I'm sure I can sort something out at work. They're pretty good on compassionate leave.'

'We'll be in touch.' Ian and Eddie walked to the front door. 'Oh, is there anyone you can think of who would wish your family harm?' Ian asked as if it was an afterthought.

Anna, who had accompanied them, held open the heavy wooden door. She stared at them. It was obvious the thought had not crossed her mind until then. 'No. Absolutely not.'

No. Just as Phillip Hardy had replied when asked the same question. Know thine enemies, or was it thy? Ian couldn't remember. Unfortunately many people were not aware that they had any.

Moira and Philippa were preparing a meal when Ian returned that evening at a time far later than he had anticipated when he had left the house in the morning. He heard them laughing as he opened the kitchen door. Unusually, he felt slightly resentful of his mother-in-law's presence, he wanted to discuss his day with his wife.

'Ah, Ian, I do hope you're hungry. I think I may have overdone it,' Philippa said as she kissed his cheek. 'We've been very busy this afternoon.'

'I'm starving actually.'

'Haven't you eaten?' Moira looked at him carefully. She knew the signs. 'Bad day?'

'Not one of the better ones. Anyone ready for a drink?'

'Silly question.'

He smiled at Philippa. That was another

thing about her he liked, she enjoyed a drink herself and never criticized others even if they over-indulged, as he had done the first time he had met her because he was terrified she would try to put Moira off this older man, a lowly policeman, who wanted to marry her daughter.

Moira laid the kitchen table. Unless they had guests they rarely used the dining-room where her sewing-machine was set up on a piece of felt on the polished table. Philippa was family and preferred informality. Ian decided to talk to Moira later when her mother had gone to bed. Philippa rarely stayed up late.

They sat down to eat as soon as Ian returned with their drinks. Philippa had made one of his favourite meals, a boiled bacon joint with onion sauce and cabbage and carrots. There was apple pie to follow. He thanked her profusely. It was a proper meal, good plain food like Moira used to cook when Mark was still at home and she didn't go out to work. He then felt obliged to join in the card game she suggested.

'So what's happened?' Moira asked when they were finally alone.

Ian outlined the details.

'Is it some sort of vendetta, do you think?'

'That's the conclusion I've been coming to but no one can suggest a reason for it. And there's still the chance these might be three separate incidents. If you ask me, it's more than enough for one family to cope with.'

'You're right, they are three very different things. Can you prove they're connected?'

'Not at the moment.' Ian stood and stretched. He was ready for bed. It was the girl's disappearance which puzzled him most. He had left a message for Barbara Hughes, Violet Baxter's solicitor, to ring him urgently. He had not mentioned Robbie Pearce's name in case she didn't consider anything to do with his request urgent. Her secretary had told him that Mrs Hughes was in court and she didn't think she'd be back in the office until the morning.

The Met had located Janice Meek, the headmistress, at her home address and faxed through the information she had given them. It matched exactly what Robbie had said. Ian had hoped that these supposed witnesses would be more forthcoming when they were confronted with officialdom but he had been disappointed.

Brenda had had no luck either. Lorna Daniels of the address Robbie had given them was not, nor ever had been, registered as a qualified teacher. In fact, Ian decided as he cleaned his teeth, Robbie Pearce had done a damn good job, albeit unsuccessfully, to have reached the stage they were at but without their resources.

'We're having a quiet day at home

tomorrow. Going to Saxborough this morning took it out of Mum,' Moira said as Ian got into bed beside her. 'She tires more easily these days.'

'I noticed. And it won't do you any harm to relax either. This is supposed to be your holiday, too.' He put an arm around her and drew her closer. Within minutes they were both asleep.

Chapter Ten

Although Anna Pearce had not had time to begin to come to terms with the death of her mother, a part of her brain was still functioning beneath the terrible numbness. Sergeant Brenda Osborne had asked her to think very carefully about events leading up to the tragedy and now she recalled the two telephone calls Audrey had received and decided this was probably important. She picked up the telephone and dialled the number Brenda had given her. It was DC Campbell who took the call.

'I've just thought of something which happened recently,' she began. 'My mother told me she'd received a couple of nuisance calls. They came in the early hours of the morning on two consecutive nights. No one actually said anything but she thought it was odd that it occurred twice in a row. Once might simply have been a wrong number.'

'When was this?'

'Last week, Wednesday and Thursday I think it was. I said if it happened again we'd contact the telephone people.'

'And did it?'

'No. Unless she didn't say because she

131

didn't want to worry me.'

'Did your mother try dialling 1471?'

'Yes, but both times the number was withheld.'

'Thank you for letting us know. We'll certainly look into it.' Alan made a note to have the calls traced. Perhaps Audrey Field had been awake when the intruder arrived, maybe she had received another call or wasn't able to sleep if she was anticipating one. But it still didn't explain the gag and the rope. It seemed that whoever broke in was expecting, possibly even wanting, to be disturbed. When the rest of the team arrived Alan passed on the latest piece of information. He had already spoken to a supervisor at BT who had promised to treat the matter as priority.

A lengthy discussion of the Pearce family's problems brought forth no conclusions. Even Ian could only come up with the theory that 'someone has it in for them', which, as he pointed out himself, was neither useful nor likely to get them anywhere. 'Why target them all? If someone bears a grudge it's usually against one person.'

'True. And Hardy might be close to them but he isn't a relative,' Short added. 'And take Audrey Field's house, it's the same story as the arson attack, no evidence, no prints. There're no flies on our man, whoever he might be.' He glanced at his watch. 'I'd better be off, the PM's scheduled for ten. I won't be eating liver for a while.'

Brenda groaned. She could just about put up with his clichés but why did he always have to make comments like that, smiling as if they hadn't all heard them before, as if he'd come up with something new?

'Nice day for it, though.' He nodded towards the window where the vertical slatted linen blinds kept out the fierce glare of the sun. 'Anyone fancy taking my place? No? Well, I didn't think so.'

Whistling tunelessly he set off down the corridor and took the lift the one floor down to the ground.

Peter Barnard was waiting for him in the mortuary at Rickenham General Hospital. Laid out on the stainless steel table was Audrey Field. Short shuddered at the sight of her naked body, not that it revolted him, it was what was about to happen to it that caused his reaction.

'We're all ready,' Barnard said as he tried not to smile. He knew how the smell affected them, these policemen who had to come to watch. It wasn't that unpleasant, more clinical than anything else, and the place was fully air-conditioned. The smell simply acted as a reminder of what they were about to witness. He thought it strange that so many showed the discomfort displayed by John Short when they saw such

133

awful and often worse things in the course of their careers.

Barnard and his assistant got to work. The more senior man dictated his findings into the microphone suspended above the body on the table. Short, notebook in hand, wrote nothing. There was nothing to write; no injuries that they hadn't seen for themselves, no signs of major surgery or scarring, nothing at all to suggest anything other than what the pathologist had suspected from his examination: Audrey Field's heart had simply stopped beating. Her GP had confirmed that he wasn't treating her for anything and that he rarely saw this patient. Her age was given as seventy-eight but she had looked much younger.

The stomach contents and blood samples would be analysed but Short realized the results would be unhelpful. She hadn't been poisoned nor was she on any medication. Knowing what she had eaten for her last meal would not help them find whoever they were looking for.

'It seems as if he wore gloves,' Barnard said. 'As far as I can tell from the fingernail clippings they're perfectly clean apart from these minute fibres which may or may not be leather. And from the shape of the bruising around her wrists it looks as if she struggled against the rope.'

'So if she was overpowered immediately

then we're not looking for someone with scratches on their face. That bloody well narrows it down, doesn't it?'

'You won't get a shot of bourbon in your coffee if you take that attitude, John.'

Short returned his grin. 'Forgive me, oh great one. It's just that we're all a bit pissed off with this case and two others with no leads. And that information is for your ears only. Don't go letting the general populace know how incompetent we are... Have you nearly finished?'

'Yes. Alastair can finish off. I'll be with you in a minute. Go and wait in my office.'

'Your cubbyhole, you mean.'

Barnard went off to wash and change. He returned, clean and in fresh operating gear, to find Short reading the paperwork he'd left on his desk.

'Sorry. Old habits die hard.' Short replaced the notes and sat down. 'Any ideas on this? I certainly haven't.'

'Honestly, John, you heard what I said out there.' He turned to open a cupboard from which he took a bottle. He poured a small measure of bourbon into a cup then filled it with coffee from the filter machine. His own coffee was unadulterated. 'I'm a mortician not a detective.'

'I know that but your examination told me no more than what we knew already. I was hoping you'd have some ideas. But it's odd that she'd been tied up. It's like something from an old black and white film. Our modern villains don't do that any more. If they're disturbed they lash out or they carry knives or guns. And the rope wasn't hers, he took it with him.'

Peter Barnard sipped his coffee. 'Perhaps his intention was to frighten her rather than rob her.'

That was a good point, one he'd bring up as his own idea. 'Well, if it was, he succeeded. Frightened her to death, if you want my opinion.'

'No such thing. Her heart gave out. At her age it could've happened at any time. Odd that he didn't blindfold her, though. It doesn't appear that he was expecting her to die.'

Short thought about it. 'What would have been the point? If she disturbed him, which he seemed to be expecting as he came prepared, she would have seen him before he had a chance to blindfold her. That makes it likely it was someone she didn't know, wouldn't recognize again, which rules out one of the family. No, bugger it, it doesn't.'

Barnard raised a questioning eyebrow.

'Got my reasoning all wrong. Maybe it was one of the family and he or she was wearing a mask or a balaclava or whatever. That would also explain why her nails were clean. Make sure you get back to us quickly with the findings on the nail clippings, Peter.'

'I'll thank you for not trying to teach me my job.' Barnard quite liked Short but he wondered how his fellow officers put up with him on a full-time basis.

'Sorry, mate. Thanks for the coffee, I'd better be going.' As he drove back to the station he wondered if any of the few stray hairs picked up from the kitchen floor would prove to be useful. If they belonged to someone other than a member of Audrey's family or one of her friends it would be something to go on if they were ever lucky enough to find a suspect. If they came from Anna or Robbie or Phillip Hardy it wouldn't mean a thing. Guilty or not, all three would have entered that cottage on numerous occasions.

'Sir, there's a Barbara Hughes on the line for you.'

'Put her through.' Ian smiled at Greg Grant. This was the call he had been waiting for. He had told her secretary it was an urgent matter yet the woman had waited until almost eleven o'clock to ring him. 'DCI Roper,' he said rather gruffly.

'Good morning, Chief Inspector. I'm sorry I couldn't get back to you sooner but I've only just got into the office. My husband was taken into hospital early this morning.'

'I'm sorry to hear that. How is he?'

'I'm not sure yet. They're doing some tests. Anyway, how can I help you?'

Ian forgave the solicitor her tardiness. He would have put Moira's welfare before returning a telephone call. 'A young man by the name of Robert Pearce came to see you recently. I wondered if you'd heard from the woman he's trying to trace.'

'Ottie Halmer. No. She left a forwarding address and a telephone number with her own solicitor. I've tried ringing it several times but there's been no answer so I've now written to her. Why is this so important? I can understand Mr Pearce's concern – how dreadful to be literally jilted at the altar – but it isn't a crime.'

'Obviously I can't go into details but it is to do with a case we're working on. I can tell you that as far as we know Ms Halmer hasn't committed any crime but she may be able to help us in tracing someone else we're looking for.'

'Goodness, two people missing at once – the girl and Miss Halmer. Well, all I can do is to give you the address and telephone number. If she replies to my letter, what do you want me to do? I have asked her to address any letter to Mr Pearce care of my office.'

'Then obviously the letter must be handed over to him. He'll contact us, I'm sure, if it contains anything relevant to us.' Ian wrote down the information he was given, thanked her and said he hoped her husband would soon recover.

He stared at the piece of paper. Colorado. For a split second he wondered if police funds would run to sending him out there to interview Ottie Halmer but whimsical dreams wouldn't get him anywhere. He now needed to contact someone on the other side of the Atlantic. It would be the middle of the night there but as in all police stations there would be officers on duty. He got Greg to find out the number he required and made the overseas call.

'They're going to go round to the apartment in the morning. If there's no joy there they'll contact the hospital where she's taken a post and come back to us as soon as they know anything,' Ian told his team when he'd ended the call. 'Let's hope they get somewhere quickly. Right, I want to make a start on the wedding guests. Have we confirmed their addresses?'

'Yes.' Brenda had been working on this. Those on the Pearces' side were mainly local. The exceptions were Don Shearwood, Robbie's best man, and his wife and child who had travelled up from Somerset, and Richard and Amanda Pearce and their two small daughters. Richard was Robbie's cousin, the son of his father's brother. He and his wife and family lived in Sheffield. It was unlikely any of them could help the police to find Lorna Daniels but they still had to be questioned. More interesting would be hearing what Lorna's guests had to say. There were six of them and they all lived in London. Ian knew the Met would be as thorough as themselves in conducting the interviews even though it wasn't their case, but Ian hoped Superintendent Thorne would grant permission for himself or one of his team to go.

Brenda, Short and Eddie Roberts were despatched to the homes or workplaces of those guests who lived in or near Rickenham Green.

'Total waste of time, that was,' Short commented without rancour when the drinks had been ordered and served. After another fruitless day they had, without prior arrangement, found themselves in the Three Feathers, a shabby pub at the top end of the High Street where, for some reason unknown to anyone, they tended to gather after work. There were far nicer places in which to drink, places with carpets which weren't greasy, where the decor was not reminiscent of a bygone age, where it felt safe to breathe the air. But the Feathers it was because it always had been so.

Brenda sipped a Campari and soda, Short slurped his Guinness, Alan Campbell had a lager in front of him as yet untouched and Greg Grant slowly poured a bottle of Mackesons. Ian, believing himself to be in the wastelands because there was no real ale, had to settle for a bottle of Newcastle Brown. 'Well, none of us believed Pearce's guests would give us a lead. Now we can have a crack at those invited by the blushing bride.' At least, she ought to be blushing, Ian thought. Tomorrow Brenda and Scruffy Short would be off to London. Not only had Mike Thorne cleared it with the Met, he had suggested that two of them go. This, Ian realized, was not because he believed it was worth that much manpower but because two officers could complete the task in a day thus saving the expense of an overnight stay.

Short leered at Brenda through his foam-laden moustache. 'I'm looking forward to tomorrow. Just the two of us. How about you?' he asked loudly over the noise of other conversations and the jukebox.

She ignored him and turned to Alan. 'When do you think the telephone people will come back to you?'

'Tomorrow, hopefully. The supervisor I spoke to said she'd give it priority.'

Greg Grant was disappointed he hadn't been chosen to go to London. He had

141

finally become used to living alone and although he still missed his dead wife he had settled into the job and now felt ready to allow a little more into his life. A day away from Rickenham Green would have suited him. However, he said nothing and was merely pleased that this team, who had worked together for so long, had accepted him so readily.

Eddie Roberts had gone straight home. He had listened to their teasing with good humour but couldn't be persuaded to join them. He wasn't a great drinker and he liked to spend time with his family. He was sure the Chief would be happy to drink his share of beer.

It was Eddie who had spoken to Robbie's cousin's wife, Amanda Pearce, over the telephone. She had never met Lorna, neither had her husband, and the little they knew of her had come from Robbie over the telephone. 'We haven't been to Little Endesley for over two years,' she'd told Eddie. 'Now we've got the girls Richard works hard to make ends meet and he's so tired at the weekends that, although they're his only relatives, I don't feel it's fair to insist he visits his aunt or Robbie in London.' She was, she'd continued, hoping to get a full-time job once her second child started school.

Eddie, realizing the conversation was

going nowhere, ended it by thanking her for her time.

It had been the same with Don Shearwood. Greg Grant had reached him on his work number. Like the cousins, he had never met Lorna. Pressure of work, a young son and a baby on the way as well as the matter of distance had kept him and Robbie apart although they remained in touch by phone. 'I've known Robbie since the day we both started at university – what's that? – roughly eight years now. I've never known him so enthusiastic about a girl and when he rang to say Lorna had agreed to marry him he sounded so very, very happy. This has devastated him. I just don't understand it. I'm so sorry I can't help you. I really wish I could.' Greg had decided it wasn't worth bothering his wife who had not met Lorna either.

All the local guests had now been questioned in person. They were either friends of Robbie's since schooldays or friends of his mother. Most of them had met his fiancée at some point during her various visits. Their stories might have been scripted, they were all so similar. Lorna was a lovely girl, Lorna always had a smile, Lorna adored Robbie and loved his family. Something must have happened to her for her not to have turned up. What they didn't know was that Lorna Daniels had lied about where she had lived although she had managed to take Robbie to the house in question on many occasions. How, and why, were the questions that needed answering. But they wouldn't know that until Ottie Halmer was found. They all wondered if this woman was somehow involved in the deception, although in what way and for what reason it was impossible to guess at. Tomorrow, hopefully, they might come a little nearer the truth.

It was Brenda who left first. She wanted to go home, have a long shower and a glass of wine and cook dinner with Andrew as they discussed their respective days. Maybe sometime in the future she would get used to being with a man who was willing to share every part of his life with her as she was willing to share hers with him. And as he had known John Pearce he would be interested in hearing how things were going. 'See you in the morning,' she said as she swung her bag over her shoulder.

'Can't wait to get your leg across, I suppose. Lucky old Andrew,' Short called out as she reached the door. But he failed to embarrass her even though many heads turned her way.

'Absolutely right,' she said with a wide smile. 'And lucky old me.'

'Another one?' Short, recognizing defeat, gestured towards Ian's empty glass. He'd stay there all night if he had company.

'One more, if you insist.'

'One more? We've only had the one. And I wasn't insisting. If anyone else wishes to purchase the next round I certainly won't stop them. Alan, how about you?'

'Thanks. I think I will.' He did not see the glances which passed between the three other men. Alan Campbell was a loner but if he did join them he made little attempt at conversation, seeming happier just to listen. On the other hand, just listening was often an asset in the job.

Greg Grant had already pushed his glass towards the barman. He was more than happy to spend a little longer in the pub for this would delay the time before he had to return to his empty house.

Their glasses refilled, the conversation turned to more general topics. When a case was over it was different, they would relive it several times over the course of the evening. For now there was nothing to say.

Ian glanced at the clock behind the bar and felt a twinge of guilt. He ought to have gone straight home to entertain Philippa and relieve Moira of some of the burden. Not, he thought, that anyone could accuse Philippa of being one, but Moira was used to her own company and having someone around for a week could be a strain on anyone.

'I've made all the funeral arrangements,' Anna said. Phillip sat beside her at the kitchen table holding her hand. Sunlight flooded the room although it was still early morning. They could smell the coffee as it percolated and the yeasty aroma of bread as it browned in the toaster. Phillip had stayed the night, sleeping beside Anna, holding her as she cried for the very first time.

'I know, darling.' She had told him last night that it was to take place next Wednesday. Five days to go. 'Is Robbie up?'

'Yes, but he's gone out. He wasn't in his room when I got up.'

Robbie had elected to stay with Anna until Sunday evening when he would return to London ready to start work on Monday. He now knew that the police were trying to trace Ottie Halmer so was not worried about missing a call from Barbara Hughes. Chief Inspector Roper would keep him informed.

'It's the waiting. For Robbie as well as for me,' Anna continued. 'It's as if we can't tie up the loose ends. I know it probably sounds callous, as if I can't wait to get rid of my mother, but I feel she's in limbo at the moment. Does that make any sense to you?'

'Of course it does. Anna, always remember how much I love you. I feel useless at the moment but if there's anything you need, anything you want me to do, then I'll do it.'

Phillip feared that with all that had taken place over the past couple of weeks he was in danger of losing Anna. It was as if something evil had touched their lives and was trying to destroy them. If it was within his power he wouldn't let it happen.

They heard the front door open. Seconds later Robbie appeared holding some envelopes. 'The post,' he said unnecessarily as he handed them to his mother.

Anna glanced at the envelopes then slit them open mechanically. Life did go on, how true that was. There were bills to be paid and junk mail to bin. Phillip had been wonderful. It was he who saw to the plumber when he arrived on Thursday afternoon. Anna hadn't felt able to face a stranger.

She flicked through the envelopes. One was plain white with her name and address neatly typed above the correct postcode. Inside was a single sheet of paper. On it were typed five words: *Phillip was sleeping with Lorna.* Anna gasped. Her face was white. Her hand shook as she placed the note in front of Phillip and watched his face as he read it. For a fleeting second she believed it was true. It would explain the girl's last-minute change of mind. But surely Phillip was too honest, too decent for that to have happened.

'Dear God, whatever next?' His outrage was apparent by the way he spoke the words. And he was shocked, Anna could see that.

'What is it?' Robbie stood behind the chair and read the note over Phillip's shoulder. 'Is it true?' he asked quietly.

'Robbie, how can you even ask?' Phillip said very quietly. He was right. Someone was trying to tear this family to pieces and his chance of happiness with it. He knew, deep down, that even if Anna and Robbie believed him the seeds of doubt had been sown. He felt like throwing himself into Anna's arms except now, more than ever, he had to be strong. 'We'll take it to the police. I suppose it would be better for them to come and collect it. Fingerprints and all that.'

'You ring them, Phillip. I'm not sure I can take any more.' Anna left the room and Robbie followed her. Neither of them wanted to hear those five words spoken aloud.

All thoughts of breakfast were completely forgotten.

Chapter Eleven

Roughly an hour before Anna Pearce received the distressing letter, Brenda Osborne and John Short had started their journey to London.

The wedding guests on Lorna's side had all been contacted. Making an appointment to see them was to give warning, a chance to think up a story if they were involved in Lorna's disappearance, but it had been necessary. The trip to London would have been wasted if any or all of them had either been ill or away on their summer holidays.

They went in one car. The addresses they were to visit were relatively close to one another. Brenda drove while Short ate a sausage sandwich, his breakfast, which he had insisted they stop for on the way out of Rickenham. When he had finished he wiped his hands on the inadequate paper serviette which had come with it and settled down to read the paper. Despite their early start they failed to avoid the city's rush-hour traffic.

In north London they stopped to check directions. 'I'll drop you at the Davies' place and come back for you when I'm done,' Brenda said.

'That's fine. If I get finished early I'll wait for you in the street.' Short glanced out of the car window. It was humid, far more so than in Rickenham Green. The sky was a perfect arc of high, pearly cloud which blocked out the sun but promised no relief in the form of rain. Short was sweating and Brenda could smell it. She wondered if he'd ever heard of deodorant.

Half a mile further on she dropped him at the end of the street and drove to the next address on the list.

Beverley Jones was a nurse. It was her day off.

Brenda selected the relevant buzzer and pressed it then waited for someone to come to the door. The woman who opened it was in her twenties and looked as if she had dressed in a hurry. Around her unmade-up face hung a mass of fair, curly hair. It was not her natural colour; darker roots were beginning to show. Her looks were average, she was neither plain nor beautiful. 'Come in,' she said. 'You'll have to excuse the mess, we had a bit of a late night.'

Brenda followed her across the wide hallway and through the door of the ground-floor flat. The windows in the spacious lounge were wide open but the room retained the smell of stale cigarettes and beer. On every surface rested sticky glasses and used paper plates. But sprawled on the settee was one of the most handsome men Brenda had ever seen. Bare-footed, bare-chested, dressed only in jeans, he seemed totally at home, so at home he did not bother to stand to greet her when she introduced herself.

'I'm Danny Maguire,' he said. 'You were due to see me later but as I stayed here last night I didn't think it was worth going home to wait for you.'

'That's fine.' Time would be saved but had the couple a reason for providing a united front?

'Can I get you some coffee?' Beverley hovered in the doorway as though she was the guest.

'No thanks.' Brenda sat down although neither had yet invited her to do so. She had no intention of questioning them on her feet. The armchairs matched the settee and the other soft furnishings. Tidy, the room would be pleasant to sit in. 'As you know, Lorna Daniels did not turn up on her wedding day. We are now trying to locate her. You said over the phone that you haven't seen her since before that day, but have you any idea where she might have gone?' The question was addressed to Beverley who had now also sat down. This information could have been gleaned over the phone but they all knew how important it was to gauge a witness's reactions.

'I'll go first,' Danny said before she could speak. He sat up and leaned forward, his hands on his knees. Brenda tried not to stare at his muscular chest. 'I've never met Lorna. All I can tell you is that she's a friend of Bev's but her invitation included a friend or partner. Naturally Bev invited me.' He grinned. 'I say naturally because we're moving in together in a fortnight. Anyway, I don't know a thing about her other than she didn't show up that day.'

'Thank you. And what about you, Bev, can you help at all?' Brenda hooked her hair behind her ears ready to start taking notes.

'We only met about a year ago. It was by chance, in a café. It was busy and we had to share a table. We got talking and it went on from there. Now and then we'd meet for a drink. We got on really well. You know how it is, something just clicks. But we both had busy lives. She's a teacher and what with my shifts and both of us having boyfriends we didn't get the chance to meet very often.'

'Where does she live?'

Beverley looked surprised. 'I don't really know. I mean, around here somewhere, obviously, but I don't know her exact address. She told me she'd got a decent place in St John's Wood.'

'Did she ever come here?'

'Only once. It wasn't that sort of friendship. I can't explain it really. As I said, we got on very well but somehow I knew we both didn't want the relationship to progress beyond the occasional drink or meal. And I was surprised when she invited me to her wedding, especially when I saw the church was in west London. It's odd, really, Lorna never met Danny and I never met Robbie, not until, well... The poor man, he must feel terrible.'

'Why are you so keen on finding her? It isn't a crime to change your mind.'

It was Danny who asked. Brenda had wondered how soon the question would occur to one or the other of them. There was nothing for it, she had to use a cliché, a Shortism. 'We think she can help us with a crime we are investigating.'

'Ah,' Danny said with a knowing smile.

'Did Lorna mention any relatives, any friends she might have gone to under the circumstances?' For surely there would be some psychological effect on Lorna, too, no matter what her motive had been; no matter that she had lied and that the choice had been hers. Not to turn up for your own wedding was no small thing.

'No relatives that I know of. She did tell me that she was illegitimate, an only child, and that her mother had died in a car crash a couple of years ago. As for friends, she talked about two named Linda and Sally, people she'd met at evening classes. They were at the reception.'

A car crash. Robbie had mentioned that, too. It might be worth checking out. At least the accounts given by Robbie and Beverley regarding the mother tallied so far. 'What evening classes?'

'Computer studies. At the local college. You know, adult education classes.'

This was something else to check. Other people there would know Lorna, even if only vaguely, and her tutor would surely have an address for her. Brenda felt as if she'd struck gold. Of course, had they asked Robbie he could have told them this. But Robbie hadn't known where she lived, perhaps he was also unaware of the classes. The term had ended but, hopefully, the tutor hadn't decided to take off for the whole of the summer holidays.

Feeling there was nothing more to be learned and that she had more than enough information to work on, Brenda decided it was time to leave.

Beverley showed her to the door. 'You don't think something's happened to her, do you?' Her face showed genuine concern.

'We don't know,' Brenda answered honestly.

'Will you let me know? Either way?'

'Yes, of course.' She walked back to where she had left the car, got in and started the engine. Depressing the button which controlled the windows she felt the stirring of a breeze as they slid open. As she pulled away her hair was lifted from her neck. The coolness was welcome and soon no traces of the Inspector's body odour or his sausage sandwich remained.

Scruffy Short was sitting on the low wall of someone's tiny front garden. One thumb was hooked into the neck of his brown suit jacket which hung over his shoulder. As she came to a stop Brenda could see the rings of sweat around the armpits of his mustard shirt. It would not be a pleasant journey home.

'How did it go?' he asked as he lowered himself into the passenger seat.

Brenda told him as they made their way to their next destination. 'And you?'

Caroline and Peter Davies were a newly married couple who lived in a neat but small town house. It was the best they could afford but they hoped to move up the property ladder as their careers progressed.

'They're Yuppies,' Short proclaimed with disgust, resorting to yet another of his outdated phrases. 'Anyway, she's in local government and he works for an advertising agency. They don't want kids for at least ten years. You should've been there, Bren, you'd think I'd been sent to write their biography. They'd both taken the morning off because they didn't want to be interviewed at work.

The likes of them not wanting to be associated with the likes of us, I suppose.'

Brenda knew there were many such people, and not only criminals. Even the innocent had a fear of contamination, as if guilt was catching. She also knew she did not like to be called Bren but to mention this would be to ensure the abbreviated use of her name for evermore.

'Davies only met Lorna once, and then only briefly, so he wasn't any help. His wife said she met her for the first time at Linda Johnson's house.'

'As in our Linda Johnson?' They were stopped at traffic lights. Brenda turned to look at him.

'Indeed, the very same. The next on the list. Linda's a secretary in Caroline Davies' department at work. I'm surprised she mixes with a mere secretary. Don't look at me like that, I'm only looking at it from her point of view. You feminists are bloody touchy.'

'Likewise you chauvinists. And I'm not a feminist. I just believe in equal opportunities and equal pay.'

'You obviously don't know the real meaning of the word or you'd realize you were paying me a compliment.'

'I do know the meaning, as it happens, not that I think being called a bellicose patriot is much of a compliment. I was simply using the modern vernacular.'

Short smirked. He enjoyed winding Brenda up. 'To continue, my lovely. Caroline Davies said Lorna seemed very keen to make new friends. She was still recovering from the death of her mother and was trying to make some changes in her life. Caroline didn't know much about her and although she claimed she liked Lorna she didn't have much room in her life for her. Too busy clambering up the social ladder, I shouldn't wonder. Like your Bev, she was surprised to have been invited to the wedding and was even more surprised there were to be so few guests. And she imagined there'd be at least one teacher present, a fact we missed. To sum it up, she was bugger all help. Let's hope we have more luck this time.' Short leaned back against the seat and folded his arms. The movement allowed a whiff of sweat to reach Brenda's nostrils. 'I'd love to have been at the so-called reception. It appears that the absence of the bride did more to break the ice than any amount of free booze. No one had any idea why Lorna didn't turn up. According to Caroline, Lorna made Robbie sound like an Adonis with brains and a sense of humour.'

'If she really felt like that it could be that she's dead.'

'Hmm. Maybe.'

They were both aware that no unclaimed corpses had turned up, none that fitted Lorna's description, although that didn't mean the body hadn't been hidden successfully. But there was still the question of her deception concerning her address.

They each had one more call to make. Short was to speak to Linda Johnson, Brenda was seeing Sally Rivers. It looked as if they would be back in Rickenham Green earlier than they had anticipated, something for which Brenda would be extremely grateful.

Ian watched as the fax rolled out of the machine, impatient for the message to end. He tore off the sheet and began to read. Ottie Halmer's US address and telephone number had been verified, as had her appointment at the hospital. She was due to take it up at the beginning of September. Her contract was for three years and, aside from her excellent references, her future employers said she was a well-respected medical researcher and could be guaranteed to attract funding wherever she worked. She was single and had a mother and brother who lived in Germany. But no one knew where Ms Halmer was. She had taken up residence in her apartment then gone off on an extended tour. Both neighbours and hospital administrators had confirmed she had told them she was touring and wanted to see as much of America as possible before she got down to work in case her contract was not renewed and she didn't have another chance. She had mentioned staying with friends along the way but no one knew who they were or where they lived.

'Damn and blast it,' Ian cursed. It could be weeks before she was traced.

The fax went on to ask how urgent the matter was and did they want Ottie Halmer located immediately? Ian knew just how much work this would entail in so vast a country and that success would be virtually impossible. Even though there was no certainty a crime had been committed, no certainty at all that the Halmer woman could help them, Ian knew they needed to talk to her. He would discuss it with Superintendent Thorne. Ian wasn't sure how their American counterparts worked but they might be able to put out a bulletin on local television stations asking her to come forward, although God only knew how many such stations existed.

Before he could ring Thorne's secretary to see if he could spare a few minutes Alan Campbell, the telephone clamped to his ear with his shoulder, gestured for him to hold on a minute. 'We'll send someone over as soon as possible,' he concluded. 'The Pearces again,' he said when he had hung up.

'Anna Pearce has received an anonymous letter claiming that Hardy was having an affair with Lorna Daniels.'

'What?' Ian's eyes widened. Was this what it was all about?

Alan shrugged, his pale, freckled face impassive. 'She's adamant there's no truth in it.'

Even so, Ian thought, the damage will have been done. There would always be the hint of suspicion. With what Anna had been through already she was, whatever she said, likely to believe the worst. As, no doubt, would Robbie Pearce. 'Postmark?'

'Indecipherable, apparently. Who do you want to go, sir?'

'I think I'll go myself. I need to speak to the Super first. Meanwhile I want you to look into the arson attack at Hardy's place again. Cover it from every angle no matter how unlikely it may seem. Whoever did it has to live here or to have been here at the relevant time. And find out exactly what young Robbie was doing that night. If his potential stepfather was having it off with his wife-to-be it's a damn good motive for damaging his property.' He turned to DS Grant who was collating evidence on all local breaking and entering cases over the past year. None, so far, had involved the use of a rope and a gag. 'I know you're busy, Greg, but have you had a chance to see what's doing with that stabbing incident?'

'Yes. Dennis Suitor seems to have developed permanent amnesia regarding that particular night and following morning, and Dave Johnson has now made a statement in which he says it was an accident. I think we can say that it's end of story.'

'Don't you start.'

'Sir?'

'You've only been here five minutes and you're already starting to sound like Scruffy Short.' He ran a hand through his springy hair. It was a sign of exasperation. Nothing would happen to Suitor now. With a witness, the main witness, Johnson, not wishing to take it further, the police would be wasting their time in bringing their own charges. The last couple of weeks had been more frustrating than any others he could remember.

When his secretary put him on, Superintendent Mike Thorne's Brummie accent came clearly down the line. The telephone always accentuated it. Ian pictured him: smartly dressed, beautifully shaved, his bald head unashamedly free of hair, unlike the embarrassing strands Short brushed over his pate. Ian explained his dilemma with the Colorado police.

'Give me the number, Ian. If nothing comes up by this evening I'll ring them myself.' Mike Thorne was beginning to think the same way as his Chief Inspector. Too many events involving the Pearce family were cropping up. Lorna Daniels may or may not have committed a crime but they needed to find her. In order to do so they first had to find Ottie Halmer. The Met had checked the electoral roll for the relevant areas in London – St John's Wood where her friends thought she lived and Ealing where Vi Baxter now resided – but the name Lorna Daniels did not appear on either.

'Thank you, sir.' Ian replaced the receiver then left the building, pleased to note that the temperature had dropped by a few degrees. The roses in the built-up beds at the front of the station were drooping and a few petals lay scattered on the parched soil. He wondered how the flowers survived when he had never seen anyone water them. Hopefully the weather was changing. Heat waves were all right for limited periods but he enjoyed the changeability of the English climate. Why people chose to retire to Spain or Portugal was beyond him. There were foreigners as well as the heat to contend with there.

He drove through the town and turned on to the minor road which led to Little Endesley. Beneath the trees which arched over the road it was cool and pleasant. He didn't see another car for over a mile.

The front door of Mulberry Cottage stood

open, as did most of the windows of the house. The curtains stirred in the gentle breeze which had risen from nowhere. 'Hello?' he called into the cool, empty hallway, feeling it was silly to knock when the door was wide open.

Anna came out of the room to his right. She was very pale and drawn. 'Thank you for coming. I just don't know how much more we can take, Chief Inspector. I really don't know who'd want to do this to us.'

'May I see the letter?'

'Of course. Do come in.'

He followed her to the kitchen at the back with its lovely view of the garden. Through the open windows the sound of rustling leaves could be heard. Far in the distance were darkening clouds. He could smell something lemony and guessed it came . from the shrub planted near the kitchen window in which at least half a dozen bees were collecting pollen. It was far too peaceful a setting for so much grief.

Anna indicated an envelope and a sheet of paper which lay on the table. 'I opened it and read it then gave it to Phillip before we realized we shouldn't have handled it so much. Robbie didn't touch it, though, and we haven't touched it since.'

Ian read the note then put on gloves and placed both it and the envelope in a plastic evidence bag. The postmark on the envelope was blurred but not badly so. With the aid of a magnifying glass it would probably be readable.

'It isn't true, you know, what it says.' Tears filled Anna's eyes. 'Even if I didn't know him as well as I do, I would swear to that. Phillip's never had the opportunity to be alone with Lorna and he certainly wouldn't ... well, you know.'

Ian didn't know. If people were determined they would make the opportunity but he didn't want to add to her pain by saying so. 'Is Mr Hardy around?'

'No. He's gone over to his house. The builders are starting today. Oh, dear, are you going to have to question him? He feels bad enough already.'

'I'm afraid I have to,' Ian replied gently. There might be something in it. If there was, Hardy was unlikely to admit to an affair in front of Anna or Robbie. 'How do you think Robbie took it?'

'He was shaken, but he doesn't believe it any more than I do.'

Doesn't? Or doesn't want to? Ian decided to see Hardy at once.

He finally got home a few minutes after seven. Moira was in the garden, a watering-can in her hand but she wasn't using it, she was looking up at the sky. 'Is it worth it?' she asked when she saw Ian come around the side of the house. Philippa had gone home that lunchtime giving Moira the rest of the day to herself.

'They forecast rain.'

'Since when did that ever mean anything? I think I'll leave it for now. Let's have a drink.'

This was their usual ritual if they were both home reasonably early. They would sit at the kitchen table with a white wine for Moira and a beer for Ian and chat and unwind before they ate. Ian poured the drinks and handed Moira a glass. Something was cooking in the oven; whatever it was, it contained garlic and made him feel hungry. Over the years Moira had gradually weaned him off the meals he had been brought up on, what he called good, plain English food. His tastes had changed. Now he actually enjoyed pasta and Chinese and Indian food and even the occasional salad.

'Michelle's getting married. It's all weddings, as you said. Or did I say that?'

Ian smiled. After so many years their thoughts had become attuned and they often both thought or said the same thing simultaneously. He had no idea how his wife managed to retain her girlish looks and could still get away with wearing tight jeans and T-shirts. Tonight her pale hair was tied back in a pony-tail.

'To Tony, I assume? And about time, too.'

Michelle worked with Moira in the office of the car showrooms. She and Tony had lived together for nine years. Ian was old-fashioned in his views on cohabitating. 'I take it we'll receive an invite.'

'I hope so. I like them both. The wedding's in October.'

And I bet it'll be a Saturday when Norwich are at home, he thought. The fact that he supported Norwich rather than Ipswich was something he had learned to keep to himself. He picked up the paper and began to read as Moira shelled peas.

'Talking of weddings, have you found your missing bride?' she asked.

'No. And there's been another develop-ment.' He told her about the letter.

'Could it be that this Lorna is responsible, especially if she's after Phillip Hardy?'

'For what?'

'Well, for all of it. She knows the family well, each of them's been hurt, badly hurt. Perhaps she wanted revenge for something she couldn't have.'

They had looked at that angle but it seemed a bit extreme. Short, of course, had come up with the one about a woman scorned. He and Brenda had reported their findings. Beverley Jones had been the most helpful and now they might get a lead through Lorna Daniels' evening class tutor. The Met might even have spoken to her by

166

now. In view of this, Thorne had decided to hold off calling Colorado until he saw what they came up with.

Linda Johnson and Sally Rivers only knew Lorna through the classes. They, too, had been very surprised to receive invitations to the wedding. DC Eddie Roberts had spoken to Robbie over the phone. Robbie knew about the classes but not where they were held. 'It was her night for herself,' he had said. 'Afterwards she and some of the others would go for a drink.' He hadn't mentioned it before because he didn't think it was important. Now it could be their only lead. And they needed to find Lorna Daniels before something worse happened.

What would Monday bring? Ian was impatient to know. Soon they would hear from the telephone people and perhaps discover who had made those night-time calls to Audrey Field. And what of Lorna's mother? Perhaps her daughter had lived with her. If so they would have an address from which to start. He had assigned someone to find out the details of the accident. Those, too, should be on his desk by Monday. He was tempted to go in in the morning but it wouldn't be fair to Moira who looked forward to having him all to herself. At least, he hoped she did. But I won't, he decided, not unless someone calls me in.

Moira poured boiling water over the peas

and put the saucepan on a ring. 'It'll be ready in a few minutes,' she said. She sighed. She could see the signs. Even if Ian remained at home all weekend his thoughts would be at work. Now that he had decorated the main rooms there was nothing for him to do. In which case I'd better think of some way of keeping him entertained, she thought. A trip out somewhere, never mind that in the peak of the season everywhere would be busy and Ian didn't like the heat.

Then, as if some force was on her side, she heard the first patter of rain against the kitchen windows and smiled to herself. Her real-ale-drinking, quirky husband would prefer to go out in wet weather when he believed everyone else would have the sense to stay at home.

Chapter Twelve

On Sunday morning Robbie Pearce rang Rickenham Green police station and left a message for DCI Roper saying he was returning to London and could be reached either at work or at home on Monday and Tuesday. He gave a contact number: his direct line because he didn't want to risk his secretary saying he was busy or in a meeting if anything important turned up. 'I'll be driving down on Tuesday evening for the funeral,' he added, knowing his mother would prefer him to be there the night before whether or not Phillip was spending the night with her. He hung up and watched the rain for a minute or two, hoping Wednesday would bring better weather.

Anna didn't want Robbie to leave until it was over but she didn't tell him this. He had the pieces of his own life to pick up, and work would help. She'd seen a lot of him lately and was aware that she had to get used to being on her own again, minus the daily visits to her mother. Phillip was being marvellous and she tended to forget that he had also suffered in what appeared to be some sort of persecution, although a wooden garage going up in flames could not be compared with losing her mother and a daughter-in-law within the space of two weeks. And as much as she fought it there was the niggling doubt in the back of her mind about Phillip's fidelity which had been brought on by the letter.

She had promised to see him later but she had wanted to have Robbie to herself until it was time for him to leave. Now she would face a few hours alone, the first solitary hours since Audrey had died.

She watched her son reverse the car and go down the drive. The tyres splashed up water and the rear lights looked fragmented through the rain-washed window as he braked to give her a toot and a wave. He, too, would grieve badly for his grandmother. Turning back into the house Anna caught a glimpse of herself in the hall mirror. She stopped and peered at her reflection. 'I look like an old woman,' she told herself and wondered if some make-up would help. It had seemed too much of an effort to bother lately.

As if to reflect her mood the rain continued to fall from a grey sky. It wasn't cold but Anna shivered. It wasn't over yet, she sensed that, but she prayed that no one else would get hurt.

It hit Robbie anew when he returned home

for the second time after that fateful Saturday. About now he should have been on his way back from the airport, his wife beside him as they prepared to start their lives together.

Lorna's case was no longer in the hall but in the cupboard where he had put it. 'You fool,' he muttered. 'Why on earth didn't you open it?' There might be something inside to shed light on her disappearance.

Still wearing the damp raincoat he had pulled on to walk from the car to the flat, he retrieved the case from the cupboard. It was locked. He reached for one of the screwdrivers kept on the shelf and wrenched it open. Something felt wrong as he handled the bikini lying on top of a summer dress. He threw these items on the floor. 'The bitch, the fucking bitch,' he said as his throat tightened and tears filled his eyes.

It hadn't been a last-minute decision, nothing had happened to Lorna, she had had no intention of marrying him. Beneath those three items of clothing was some screwed-up newspaper and a few ancient magazines to add weight. No wonder she hadn't bothered to return for the case. The dress was one he did not recognize, she had probably bought it in a charity shop. Just to make certain he wasn't missing anything he pulled everything out on to the floor but there was only rubbish to be found. He rang

Rickenham Green police station and left another message for the Chief Inspector then took himself out for a drink and a meal before a sense of defeat overcame him.

In the morning, only slightly hung over, he returned to work. Dave Monkton, one of his Little Endesley friends who had been at the church for the wedding, would have spread the news. Anna had asked him to do so. It would have been impossible for him to walk in to a barrage of suggestive comments and congratulatory back-slapping and then have to explain. Robbie hoped no one was insensitive enough to ask him about it. Dave had been questioned by the police but he hardly knew Lorna, all he could tell them was that she had seemed pleasant and friendly on the two occasions they had met.

And now it was time to face his banking colleagues.

DC Eddie Roberts' placid face was creased with a frown. This was unusual. Ian knew right away that, whatever he had brought up on the computer, the news was not good. 'There's no record of anyone by the name of Daniels being involved in a fatal RTA over the last four years; none that haven't been accounted for by family members. I've done a nationwide search and I've spoken to the families involved. The name Lorna Daniels didn't mean anything to any of them.'

172

Ian shook his head. 'If she was telling the truth about her parentage it wouldn't. Perhaps the girl took her father's name.' No, that didn't make sense. According to Robbie Lorna had never seen her father and her mother refused to discuss him. A woman who felt that way would not give her child her ex-lover's name. 'Maybe the accident happened abroad.'

'No. I checked with Robbie a few minutes ago. He was led to believe it happened in London. Oh, he's back at work today. He left a couple of messages yesterday.' Eddie explained about the suitcase and its contents. He wondered if this had been done to cause further pain. Lorna Daniels must surely have guessed he would open it at some point.

'Heaven knows where we go from here.' Another dead end. If anything important had come to light over the weekend someone would have been in touch with him. He'd kept his mobile on whenever he was out of the house. And out he had been. Moira had insisted they drive to the coast where, like many unfortunate tourists, they had tried to make the most of it by walking in the rain and having lunch in the dining-room of one of the smarter hotels.

DC Alan Campbell sauntered into the general office. He was eating a doughnut and there was sugar on his chin. Ian envied a man who could eat what he liked and as much of it as he wanted and yet remained lean.

'I checked Robbie Pearce's movements for the times surrounding the fire at Hardy's place. His mother confirmed that he set off for London in the early afternoon on Monday. He took a taxi from the house. That's been confirmed. Then he rang us from the station. He definitely caught the train to Ipswich because the bloke who sells the tickets knows him.'

'How?'

'He knew his father. Apparently John Pearce often travelled by train and he'd seen the two of them together. He saw him board the train because he has to go out to the platform with one of those bat things to wave it off.'

'And after Ipswich?'

'We can only assume he did go back to his flat. His mother rang him at around ten fifteen that night. It was a landline so he had to have been there at that time. About nine thirty the next morning he called on Mrs Baxter at the house where he believed Lorna to have been living. I rang her, too, and she confirmed the time. Pearce's car was at the flat so it's possible he drove back to Little Endesley, did a bit of fire lighting and returned to London again sometime during the early hours of Tuesday morning.

He had eleven hours in which to complete the return journey, although Mrs Baxter said he looked sad rather than tired. That's it. Do you want his neighbours questioned, sir?'

Ian thought about it. The Met would soon be sick and tired of them. At 00.53 the emergency services had responded to the call from Hardy's neighbour. Ian had heard the sirens as he lay in bed. That gave Robbie Pearce two and a half hours in which to make the journey from London to Little Endesley. At that time of night, with virtually empty roads, it would have been easily possible. Interviewing his neighbours in the block of flats where he lived would probably be pointless. If he left at around ten thirty they would have been watching TV or tucked up in bed. There was always the slim chance someone had seen him leaving the building but he would have made certain no one heard him return. But it was, to coin one of Short's phrases, a stone they dare not leave unturned. 'I think we'd better do it. I'll leave it to you to organize.'

Alan nodded and stuffed the remains of the doughnut into his mouth.

It was still raining but more of a drizzle now. Ian looked down on the street below. On the opposite side of the road people hurried along beneath umbrellas, folding them quickly if they were going into one of the shops in the parade which had been built at the same time as the precinct in which the police station now stood. It wasn't that many years ago but Ian could hardly remember how it had all looked before the houses that once belonged to railway workers along with the Station Hotel had been pulled down to be replaced by what he considered to be a concrete eyesore. He had to admit that compared to some urban architecture it could have been worse.

A telephone rang. 'I'll get it,' Brenda said as she slung her cream mac over the back of a chair. 'Rickenham Green CID.' She listened, made a few notes then didn't speak until her final 'Thank you.' 'It's about Audrey Field's silent calls. That was the BT supervisor, sir. The calls were made from a mobile phone, the sort you buy over the counter then pay for as you go.' They all knew that the owner would be virtually untraceable even if he or she paid with a credit card. There were hundreds of places where you could buy them and each outlet probably sold many every day. 'Anyway, I've got the number,' she said as she picked up the phone again and dialled it. There was no reply; no reply, no engaged signal, no recorded voice asking her to leave a message, nothing at all. The line was dead.

'This makes it even more serious,' Ian said

when Brenda told him. 'You're right, we'll never trace who bought it, but it seems to me that whoever did so wanted to make sure we couldn't find them. Someone here is being very, very careful.'

Several phones began ringing at once. Ian left the detectives to get on with their work and went to his office. He needed a decent cup of coffee and some time in which to think. Gina, his secretary, could be guaranteed to supply the first but his thoughts were a different matter. To form a theory, however absurd, facts or a motive were necessary. The only facts they possessed were concerning the victims and the motives were as yet unguessable.

It was DS Grant who took the call from the police in London later that morning. Lorna's tutor, Mrs Palmer, had been away for the weekend but they had now spoken to her. Because she was not an employee of the college and only worked there part-time in the evenings she kept her students' records in her briefcase which she kept with her at home unless she was teaching.

'At last,' Greg said. The address given was in St John's Wood. Now they had something definite to go on.

'What do you want us to do?' the officer at the other end of the phone asked.

'We need to question Miss Daniels ourselves. I expect my boss will get on to yours

177

to clear it sometime today. Thanks very much for your help.'

'Any time.'

The response may have been genuine but Greg thought he detected a hint of superiority in it. It wasn't their fault that half of the suspects and witnesses lived in the metropolis.

Greg rang the telephone number he had been given and asked to speak to Nigel.

'I'm afraid there's no Nigel here,' the young-sounding female voice told him.

'I'm sorry to have bothered you. I must've misdialled.' He replaced the receiver and went to speak to the Chief. 'She's at home, or somebody is. I just rang and made out it was a wrong number.'

Ian made the usual courtesy call to the Met to say that two of his officers would be interviewing a suspect in their area then sent Greg Grant and Brenda Gibbons on their way.

'At this rate it would be easier to move to the city,' Brenda commented drily as they drove off. But she felt a prickle of excitement knowing that they might be getting close.

The traffic was heavy, the journey made worse by the weather. Lorries sent up filthy spray as they sped down the A12 and an accident slowed them up for a while. When they finally reached their destination they parked the unmarked car in the street and stepped out into the rain.

It had been a change for Brenda to be driven. The Chief always left it to her unless they had a pool car with a driver, and Scruffy Short, although he normally insisted on taking the wheel, had, on her last trip to London, allowed his hunger to overcome his prejudice against women drivers.

The rain emphasized the drabness of the street. The terrace of brick-built properties had a veneer of grime and bins stood over-flowing in the basement areas. However, total neglect was not in evidence. Some windows sported white nets, matching curtains and window boxes in which flowers bloomed. Number 37 was one of the better places. The paint was fresh and the windows were clean. Brenda looked up as a movement caught her eye. A small face had appeared at an upstairs window.

Greg pressed the bell then put his hands in his trouser pockets, his neck hunched against the rain.

The front door was opened by a young woman holding a sleepy baby. Its thumb was in its mouth. Behind her a mongrel dog growled but without any ferocity. 'Yes?' She looked more puzzled than worried. 'If you're Jehovah's Witnesses then—'

'No, we're police officers.' Greg held out his identity and introduced them both.

Brenda bit her lip. How anyone could

mistake them for a couple who had come to talk religion was beyond her. And this slim young woman with her pretty but sharp-featured face and short, shaggily cut hair was certainly not Lorna Daniels. According to Robbie, Lorna was tall, her looks were more Italian than English and, as Robbie's friends had confirmed, she was beautiful.

'Has something happened to Andy?' Panic flickered in the woman's face.

'No. We're here to speak to Lorna Daniels,' Greg said in his low, reassuring voice.

'Who?'

Greg's and Brenda's eyes met. Surely not another dead end?

'Look, you'd better come in, I don't want Lucy to get another cold. She's just got over the last one.'

They followed her down the hall which was carpeted in dark blue wool. The walls looked newly painted in a lighter shade of blue. The woodwork was gleaming white. 'I'm Frankie Holland, by the way,' she said before stopping at the foot of the stairs to call out, 'I hope you're behaving yourself, Matthew. My son,' she explained in a normal voice. 'He's five and it's a job to entertain him during the holidays, especially in weather like this. He's been at school a year now. They seem to start them earlier these days.'

The kitchen was clean and tidy apart from

180

a few toys on the floor. The dog sniffed at Greg's trouser leg then slumped in its basket beside the back door.

'Have a seat,' Frankie said as she placed the baby on the floor. Lucy began to crawl towards the dog. 'Would you like some tea?'

'That would be nice.' Greg smiled. He could do with some and the woman seemed friendly enough – she would probably be prepared to help if she knew anything.

Frankie made the tea and placed the mugs on the scrubbed pine table. She reached for cigarettes and lighter which she kept on a shelf out of the reach of the children. 'I don't usually smoke when the children are around but you gave me a fright just now. I thought Andy might've had some sort of accident.' She offered them the packet before she lit up. Neither Greg nor Brenda smoked.

'Andy's your husband?' Brenda asked. Her own husband's name was, for some reason, never abbreviated.

'Yes. Look, you said you wanted to speak to someone called Laura Daniels. Who is she?'

'Lorna. Lorna Daniels. We were rather hoping you could tell us that.' Brenda smiled encouragingly.

'I've never heard of her.'

'That's odd, because she gave this as her address.'

Frankie blew smoke towards the ceiling. 'Perhaps she lived here once.'

'When did you move in?'

'I was three months pregnant with Lucy so that makes it about eighteen months ago. We've been doing it up gradually and we've nearly finished.'

'Who did you buy it from?'

'Franklyn and Co.'

'No, I meant the people who lived here at the time.' Brenda took a sip of her tea.

'Oh, I see. They were called Garfield. An elderly couple. It got too big for them and there were too many stairs. We got it at a good price because they'd really let it go and it needed a lot doing to it. Thankfully Andy doesn't mind decorating. Why are you asking? No, Lucy.' She turned to the child who was patting the dog over-enthusiastically. Lucy looked up at her mother, her lower lip trembling at the admonishment, but decided not to cry.

Greg sighed. 'We need to find Lorna Daniels in order to question her on several matters. So far she's given us two false addresses.'

Brenda frowned. Something was wrong. It would come to her in a minute, the way things did if you tried to forget them. Lorna Daniels must know the area to have given this address, the address of a house which a schoolteacher would have been able to afford. Then she remembered what it was. The telephone number. 'Did you receive a call this morning? A wrong number?'

Frankie's mouth opened with surprise. The policewoman seemed to have supernatural powers. 'Yes, I did actually.'

Greg blushed. 'I'm afraid that was me. I apologize. We believed at the time that Miss Daniels lived here and we wanted to make certain she was at home rather than make a wasted journey.'

'So she knows my number as well.'

'It would seem that way. Are you ex-directory?'

'No.'

'What about your husband, would he know who this woman is?' Brenda had to ask. She wondered if Andy Holland might know more about Lorna than merely who she was. After the way she had treated Robbie Pearce it would be no surprise to learn that she was seeing a married man and using his address as her own regardless of the consequences.

At that moment Matthew thumped down the stairs and came into the kitchen.

'Say hello,' his mother prompted as he stared at the two strangers.

He did so, shyly, then asked for some orange juice which he was allowed to help himself to from the fridge.

'To answer your question, Andy's never

183

mentioned the name but I can ask him later if you like.'

'What does he do for a living?' Greg ruffled the little boy's hair. He would have liked to have had a son but one daughter was all he and his wife had managed to produce. Now that this daughter was married he might be lucky enough to have a grandson.

'He sells private medical insurance.'

'Then she might be one of his clients. We'll need to contact him at work.'

'But how would she know where he lives?' Frankie paused. 'I see. You think... I mean, Andy wouldn't, he's not like that, and we're very happy together.'

There were times when Brenda hated parts of her job and what it could do to people. Now another woman's mind had been filled with doubt.

'Look, use my phone, ring him now, he'll be in his office.'

Greg stood and used the kitchen extension so Frankie Holland would be able to hear his part of the conversation. After briefly explaining the situation he waited while Andy Holland went to check his records.

'No, there's no such name on the computer, she's not with us. You can come and check for yourself if you like.'

'There's no need for that.' If there was anything suspicious Holland would have wiped the details before they got there.

'The name means nothing to me, I'm sorry. May I speak to my wife?'

'Of course.' Greg held the receiver towards Frankie who got up and came to the phone.

'We'll leave you in peace now,' Greg said once Frankie had finished speaking to her husband and no longer looked so upset.

The rain had stopped but it was a dull afternoon and now they couldn't fail to hit the rush-hour traffic. In the car Brenda rang her own Andrew to say she'd be late. She had one of those moments when she couldn't wait to see his familiar face but for now she had to settle for the drive back and the feeling of disappointment the afternoon had produced. They had expected to speak to Lorna Daniels, maybe even arrest her. The woman was certainly an expert in leaving false trails.

Ian was in the Crown with Moira when the call came through from Brenda from the car at five forty. Like everyone else he had believed the trip would be successful. As the afternoon wore on and there was no news he had reasoned that Greg and Brenda must have interviewed Lorna at length and that, in the end, she had nothing to answer for other than ruining Robbie Pearce's life. They were probably also checking unbreakable alibis.

Nothing had been learned from Pearce's neighbours regarding the night of the fire.

185

The few that had been at home during the day couldn't recall what they had been doing on a night two weeks previously. The rest would be interviewed that evening when they got back from work.

'Ian?'

'Sorry, I was miles away.'

'More like half a mile, back at the station.'

He grinned at her astuteness. 'What were you saying?'

'I asked if you wanted another drink. Fancy you not hearing that.'

'No need for sarcasm. Yes, if you're having another one.'

'I am. And it's a Chinese takeaway tonight, I don't feel like cooking. Oh bugger, it would be my round.'

Ian looked over his shoulder. Only then did he realize what he'd done. He hoped nobody else would notice, especially the female of the two people who were approaching them. 'Hello. I'm sure you need a drink after this afternoon's fiasco.'

Brenda and Greg looked tired and defeated, as anyone would who had had a wasted journey. Ian had just realized he had sent two sergeants, having temporarily forgotten Brenda's promotion. 'My wife's buying.'

Brenda nodded. 'She would be. Nice to see you, Moira. Have you met DS Grant? Greg, this is Mrs Roper.'

'I'm very pleased to meet you.'

'And you. But please call me Moira.' She shook his hand. So this was the widower Ian had talked about. He had a nice face and a well-modulated voice. It was good to put faces to the names of the people who worked with Ian. 'How was your honeymoon?' she asked Brenda, hoping it wasn't tactless asking in front of Greg.

'Wonderful, except it seems ages ago already.'

The drinks which Ian had ordered while the introductions were being made appeared on the bar. Moira got out her purse.

'I let Andrew know I'd be late but he's got a meeting anyway. As I'm only stopping for one, let me get the drinks.'

Feeling the need to lighten the disappointment so obvious in the faces of his officers Ian said, 'Now girls, there's no need to fight over who pays for my beer.'

Brenda looked at Moira and winked.

Chapter Thirteen

Tuesday produced nothing new. The only thing that had been achieved was that Superintendent Thorne had contacted a senior officer in Colorado who had agreed to do all he could to assist. 'We're in luck,' he told Ian. 'He's an Anglophile, he spends his holidays over here.'

'That is luck, indeed. Did you know that only about seven per cent of Americans have passports?'

Mike Thorne stared at him with surprise. John Short might be the master of clichés but his Chief Inspector had a store of strange facts.

Ian could understand the Americans' reluctance to travel. Apart from the fact that they had a huge continent of their own to explore, why should anyone wish to spend part of their hard-earned holidays at airports or in coaches amongst people whose language you couldn't comprehend? Yes, he had a passport but sojourns across the Channel were to please Moira, and they had never been further than Europe.

'I won't detain you, you'll want to be getting home.'

Ian said goodbye and left. How right Mike Thorne was. There was nothing more he could do and the day had already been a frustrating waste of time. Hopefully Ottie Halmer would be found quickly.

Barbara Hughes, the Baxters' solicitor, had rung to say she still hadn't had a reply to her letter but she had not known what Ian knew, that Ms Halmer was touring. So many negatives, Ian thought as he made his way home under a clear blue sky. For once there was a parking space right outside his house. He took this as an optimistic sign.

That evening Robbie Pearce set off for Little Endesley. His employers had not objected to his having two days off so soon after his holiday. To have his grandmother die – and in such a way – so soon after being jilted must have been a dreadful blow.

It was still daylight when he arrived at Mulberry Cottage. Birds were singing and a magpie hopped across the lawn. One for sorrow, Robbie thought, wishing it hadn't caught his eye.

Anna had been watching for him from the front room window. 'Any news from the police?' she asked as she kissed his cheek.

'No. Nothing. How're you feeling?'

'Sad, but I'm all right.'

You don't look it, Robbie thought as he followed her to the kitchen where Phillip sat going through some papers, his briefcase at his feet. 'Hello, Phillip.'

'Hi, Robbie.' Phillip tried to sound more cheerful than he felt.

All three were subdued as they ate their evening meal. They wanted tomorrow to be over with but did not say so. It would have seemed disrespectful to Audrey, as if they wanted her out of the way as quickly as possible. The inquest was not for another two weeks; another hurdle for Anna, but Phillip had assured her he'd be there.

At ten o'clock Phillip went home. He didn't feel it was right to sleep in Anna's bed the night before she buried her mother. Not long afterwards Anna and Robbie went to their rooms.

Dave Johnson had found a full-time job. From now on he was going straight. He would be respectable and he'd stay away from the Black Horse. He'd read last week's *Herald*. Things had gone wrong, terribly wrong, and he couldn't allow it to happen again. At least he'd had a chance to speak to Dennis Suitor who obviously couldn't remember a thing about that fateful night.

'I just can't believe I stabbed you,' he'd kept repeating in bewilderment. 'I'm not a violent man, you know that, Dave.'

'No hard feelings, Dennis. Best forget it.' And that had been that. Dave would keep away from Dennis, too. He didn't want to risk saying anything to him which might jog his memory.

'A job? About bloody time,' Myra had said when Dave came home with the news. But he could tell she was pleased.

Once he had started looking in earnest he realized there were still opportunities for a skilled painter and decorator. Houses always needed doing up, and the DIY superstores hadn't cornered the market entirely.

On Tuesday evening Dave and Myra sat at the kitchen table eating sausages and chips. It was one of the rare occasions when they were able to share a meal. 'What's up?' Myra asked. Dave was not normally so quiet and he hadn't even switched the TV on to watch the news. 'Job not going well?'

'No, it's fine. I'm just tired, I expect. I've only been at it less than a week and I'm not used to working an eight-hour day again.'

Myra nodded but she didn't believe him. There was something on his mind or else he was unwell. 'It's your injury,' she guessed. 'You're overdoing things before you're ready.'

'You're probably right,' he said as he got up and kissed the top of her head, an action which was as uncharacteristic as his carrying his plate to the sink which he then did. Myra wondered if he'd got another woman.

Anna had expected it to be raining, although she couldn't have explained why. People died and were buried in all sorts of weather. Just because her family was grieving didn't mean that the sun wouldn't continue to shine.

Even though protocol was more relaxed than in her mother's younger days, Anna wore black. A woman of Audrey's age would have expected it. Phillip's suit was dark blue, Robbie's grey with a thin pin-stripe. It felt odd being so formally dressed on a bright Wednesday morning.

'Are we ready?' Phillip asked quietly, noticing that the black dress made Anna's paleness even more apparent.

Together they walked the short distance to the village church. Anna had decided it was unnecessary and rather ostentatious to have the hearse go to Audrey' s house and for them to follow it in a car when the walk took less than five minutes.

DS Brenda Osborne and DC Eddie Grant sat discreetly at the back, also suitably attired for the occasion. The small church was almost full. Audrey had known a great many people. 'It's worth a try,' Ian had told them. 'At least you can watch their reactions – and if you get the chance, without being tactless, ask Mrs Pearce if there were any strangers present. And you never know, whoever's got it in for them might try to spoil the funeral.'

Seven days. It was quite a long time for the Pearces to have waited to bury Audrey Field but, as was often the case now, the living of the young vicar of Little Endesley was shared between three parishes and this was his first available date. Anna had wanted her mother buried in the place where she had been so happy, the ceremony conducted by someone she knew and liked even if her church attendances had been sporadic, and where she, Anna, could attend to her grave easily.

The organ music swelled. Anna, Phillip and Robbie turned their heads, tears filling their eyes as the pall-bearers entered the church.

The service paid tribute to Audrey, the vicar's words a pleasure to hear because he had known her and his feelings were genuine. When it was over and the gravediggers stood ready to fill in the grave the mourners made their way to Mulberry Cottage. Brenda accepted a cup of tea although she'd have preferred something stronger. Drinks were lined up on a trolley in the large front room and a table held plates of food. Across the crowded room she saw Eddie Grant balancing a cup and saucer as he conversed with a very old lady. The elderly were often a good source of information. Eddie might be asking her about Lorna Daniels.

Anna had agreed to their being in the church and understood the reason for it, although they hadn't expected an invitation back to the house afterwards. But, as the Chief had said, anything was worth a try. If asked, they were there as friends of Robbie.

It was Phillip who came over to ask if he could get Brenda something to eat. 'No, thanks, I'm not really hungry.' She was remembering her own mother's funeral. She had died in her forties when the drink had taken its toll. There had been few mourners there and those few had dispersed after the short service at the crematorium. 'Phillip, I know this isn't the ideal time for questions, but I'd rather ask you than risk upsetting Anna further. Was there anyone at the church, or is there anyone here now, that you don't know or weren't expecting?'

'No.' He paused to give himself time to think. 'No, I'm certain. There's just us, John's family who are only really here to support Anna and Robbie – they hardly knew Audrey – and people from the village.'

'Thank you. I'm sorry I had to ask.'

'No problem. I'm glad it's over, it's been such a strain for them both. If you'll excuse me I'd better go and rescue Anna.' Phillip walked over to where she was standing, a woman either side of her, both of whom seemed to be talking at once. Brenda thought they wouldn't have looked out of place knitting away at the foot of a guillotine.

Anna raised her head and smiled wanly at Philip. There was a little more colour in her cheeks than earlier but that might have been due to the glass of whisky she was clinging to with both hands like a talisman, as if it could ward off the pain.

'Brenda, do you have everything you want?'

She had not seen Robbie approaching. She sensed he felt awkward using her first name rather than her rank. 'Yes, thank you. We've been well looked after.'

'You haven't heard anything about Lorna, have you?'

'No, but the police in Colorado where Ottie Halmer's going to work have agreed to try to find her. She's touring the country unfortunately, that's why she didn't come back to the solicitor you contacted.'

'Really?' He was impressed. He had not expected his ex-fiancée's disappearance to be taken so seriously by the Americans. 'I don't suppose you've any idea how long it'll take? No. Stupid question.' He sighed. The funeral had made him forget Lorna for an hour or so.

Brenda looked for somewhere to put her cup and saucer. Anna and Robbie would feel better for a while. They would coast on the adrenalin rush of having got through the ceremony and entertained their guests. Tomorrow it would hit them again. 'I think we'd better be going.' She nodded in Eddie's direction and he, recognizing the cue, ended his conversation and joined her. They said goodbye to Anna, who would soon have to face clearing then selling her mother's house and learning to live with the strangers who took up residence there.

'Well, nothing to learn there,' Eddie said as they walked back to where they had left the car outside the church. It was hotter than ever. Ripples of heat danced over the surface of the road. The village was quiet and dusty and crickets could be heard in the hedgerow. The bitter scent of some wild flowers was released when Eddie brushed against them. Away from the small main street they might have been in an idyllic setting for a play rather than a place where people actually lived and worked. 'I threw in a few questions about Lorna. Same old thing: lovely girl et cetera. No one can really believe it happened to Robbie. How about you?'

'Likewise. I didn't learn a thing. But the more I see of them, the more convinced I am that this family isn't involved with what's happening to them.'

'So you don't go along with the theory?'

'What theory?' Brenda unlocked the car, wishing she'd left a window open. It was stifling inside. 'That it was Robbie who changed his mind about marrying and killed her rather than admit it? No, I don't go along with it. Accepted, he might have killed her but not for that reason. It's not a strong enough motive, not these days.' Their collective thoughts had now turned full circle. Lorna might have been missing since before the day of the wedding. They only had Robbie's word for it that she disappeared on that particular day. To put himself in the clear he might have gone ahead with the arrangements as planned and acted as surprised as everyone else when she didn't turn up.

'What reason then?' Eddie strapped himself into his seat-belt as Brenda started the engine.

'The usual ones: hatred, anger, a row that went seriously wrong, you know, perhaps he hit her and she fell over and landed on her head. And if there really are no relatives she wouldn't have been missed, especially as it was the end of the school year.' If she actually was a teacher, Brenda amended silently.

Eddie nodded. He was thinking. Wherever she lived or had lived there would be bills to be paid as well as rent or a mortgage. At some point the lack of payment would be noticed. But it would be weeks, possibly months before it was taken seriously as lack of payment would initially only be followed up by letters until finally a summons was served or the gas, telephone, electricity or water were cut off. 'So where did she live?'

'What?' Brenda, concentrating on the road, could not have been expected to follow his train of thought.

'She gave two false addresses but she had to live somewhere.'

'Well, not in north London according to the Met. Besides, we're not sure about the first one. Although Robbie Pearce swears he's been there many times we've only his word that Lorna told him she lived there. Who's to say it wasn't Ottie Halmer he'd gone to visit?' Robbie had been able to describe the interior with accuracy. They had checked with Mrs Baxter. 'No, he definitely didn't go into the kitchen or upstairs,' she had told them with certainty. For some reason she had not seemed surprised when asked to describe her unusually designed house. Perhaps she was becoming used to strange requests since she had moved in. However, Eddie was right, it was Lorna herself who had provided the false address for her evening class tutor and there had to be a reason for that.

'What about the wedding then? You have to fill in forms to get a licence.'

'True, but does anyone check them? Anyone can get a copy of a birth certificate and if she knew she wasn't going to turn up it wouldn't matter what address she gave.'

But it was the first thing they checked after they got back and reported another lack of success. Someone would come back to them regarding Lorna Daniels' birth certificate. Brenda waited impatiently for the information. At four thirty she relayed it to the rest of the team. 'Lorna Daniels was born in 1975. The names of both parents are recorded. They were married.' She paused to let this sink in. Lorna had told Robbie that she was illegitimate. 'And they did live in north London at the time.'

'Have we traced the parents?' Short asked.

'Not yet.' She grinned. 'Another little task for our London pals.'

'If Lorna Daniels is the girl's real name she can't have been in touch with her parents,' Greg Grant pointed out.

'What makes you so sure?'

Greg thought about it. 'Now you mention it, I'm not. They weren't at the wedding, but then they couldn't be because she'd said her mother, who supposedly brought her up alone, was now dead. It could be that they knew nothing about it and didn't need to if she didn't intend marrying.'

They were getting ready to leave when the phone on Brenda' s desk rang. 'Damn,' she muttered as she picked up the receiver. She listened for several seconds. 'Excuse me a minute.' She placed her hand over the mouthpiece. 'Don't go. We've got a break-through.' She listened again, thanked the person she was talking to and hung up.

'Well?' Ian was impatient. It was time they had some good news.

'Mr and Mrs Daniels are both alive and well. The police contacted their next-door neighbours once they discovered they'd moved. Fortunately they were good friends and knew their present address as they still meet. They still live in London. The reason they moved was to get away from painful memories. Their daughter, Lorna, died four years ago when she was twenty-three.'

Ian shook his head. They should have known, it was an old trick. All you had to do was to find a headstone in a cemetery or hear about someone your own age who was no longer living then send off for a copy of their birth certificate. It was possible the real Lorna Daniels had known the woman they were after. 'Brilliant. Okay, we now know she's using a false name, but what the hell is her real one? And I bet she only used the false one for the benefit of the Pearce family. I bet she's out there going about her daily business under her real one and laughing her head off at us. Just pray we hear something from Colorado tomorrow.'

'Just to make your day, the results are back on the anonymous letter received by Anna

Pearce,' Short announced. 'The envelope was self-seal, likewise the stamp.' Technological progress sometimes made detection harder: now they would not be able to test for saliva. 'The note was produced by a computer printer, an item easily accessible to anyone. There were, of course, fingerprints. The ones on the envelope were useless, only partials, and anyway several unknown postmen would have handled it before it reached Little Endesley. Those on the letter belonged to Anna Pearce and Phillip Hardy.' This was bad news because it implied that the sender was not just some spiteful person out to cause further pain, someone who wouldn't imagine the police would become involved. The sender had not touched the paper with bare hands so he or she probably knew that the police were already involved. And until they had a suspect any prints would have been useless anyway.

'The postmark?'

'Well, my lovely Mrs Osborne, it was, as we thought, London. North London actually.'

Short leaned back in his chair and scratched the expanse of his stomach. He belched before he spoke and rather enjoyed the reminder of bacon this produced. 'Except that if this woman who calls herself Lorna Daniels wants everyone to believe that she lives in that area it's the logical place to post a letter without being too specific.'

'I've had enough,' Ian said as he loosened his tie. He needed a shower but more than that he needed a drink.

'Who's for the pub?' Short asked as if he'd read Ian's mind, which was more than likely.

'Not me,' Brenda answered immediately. It was warm enough to eat in the garden and that was exactly what she and Andrew intended to do.

'Ah, same old thing. You just can't wait to get back to that randy husband of yours, can you?'

'I really don't know why you always have to be so vulgar.'

'Because I enjoy it. I like to see your pretty little nose wrinkle in disgust, it turns me on. Mind like a sewer, that's me.' He grinned as if this was something of which to be proud. 'Well, who's for the Feathers?'

'If you make it the Crown, count me in,' Ian said.

In the end it was just the two of them who made their way up the High Street, crossing the road when the rush-hour traffic had come to a standstill and feeling the heat of the day rising from the pavements. DS Greg Grant had thought about it and decided he couldn't keep up with the Inspector. He would have to limit his trips to the pub if he was to avoid multiple hangovers.

Ian's glass was empty in minutes. He wiped his mouth with the back of his hand.

'I needed that.' He ordered a second and they took their drinks to the window seat to gain the benefit of any draught which might flow through the open window.

An hour later, tired of discussing the Pearces and their problems, Ian decided it was time to go home.

Chapter Fourteen

Because he would need the car later, Phillip Hardy drove the short distance to his office. He parked behind the estate agency and walked around to the front to let himself in. With the lightest of breezes ruffling the leaves of the trees it was cooler than the previous day, but only marginally so and the hanging baskets looked in need of water. He would ask Justin to see to it when he arrived. Because of the display boards in the window the sun did not penetrate their working area. The upstairs had once been the living accommodation of the shopkeeper who had owned the property before Phillip's father took it over. It was now rented out to a middle-aged, single lady who managed a shoe shop in Rickenham Green. Phillip hardly ever saw or heard her. She paid her rent regularly and was an ideal tenant.

He went into the small office at the back and filled the filter machine. Unless he was staying with Anna he didn't bother with breakfast, it was she who insisted he ate something before he went to work.

It's such a waste, he thought, both of them living in large houses. The sooner he could persuade her to set a date for their wedding, the better. Anna had agreed to marry him some time ago but they hadn't wanted to break the news to Robbie and Lorna until after their marriage. 'You're right, it would steal their thunder,' Audrey had commented after expressing her delight that Philip was to become her son-in-law. She had laughed. 'Two weddings, starting with the youngest generation. Maybe it'll be my turn next.' But fate had had other things in store for her.

However, after recent events Phillip knew it would be tactless to press Anna. She needed time to grieve and it would be rubbing salt into the wound to tell Robbie of their plans so soon after the fiasco of his own wedding day.

Justin arrived and gladly got out the stepladder to water the plants which trailed from moss-lined baskets attached to the facia board by wrought-iron fittings. 'What time's this morning's viewing, Phillip?' he asked when he'd made a few telephone calls.

'Ten thirty. I'm meeting the Abbotts there.' They were a couple from the Midlands who were moving to be nearer their daughter and her family.

Justin nodded and went to fill his own mug with coffee. He drank almost as much of it as his boss. If they sold the Old Mill right away it would be great publicity as word got around quickly in the area. They had only starting advertising it a week ago.

At a quarter to ten Phillip straightened his tie, checked his hair was tidy and left. He was not a vain man but he did believe that appearances were important, that a man who looked smart would be assumed to be smart in business.

The drive took just over half an hour. The Old Mill was exactly that. For many years the water-wheel had been functionless, immobilized for safety reasons and serving only as an attractive feature in the grounds. The building where the grain had been ground was now a garage large enough to hold three cars with ease. The low, stone house was also a cheat. When hard-working men and women had lived in it there would have been sash windows and a slate or tiled roof. Today sunlight glinted off the leaded panes, and woven into the modern thatch on the roof was the shape of a water-wheel. Hooped barrels which had been cut in half and filled with flowers adorned the front of the house. It was chocolate-box rurality which bore no resemblance to what life would have been like for the original occupants. But this was the sort of place people were willing to pay huge sums of money for, people who probably believed the building to be authentic.

Phillip rapped on the door with the brass

knocker. It was opened by the elderly owner. 'Ah, Mr Hardy, you're punctual. I cannot abide tardiness. Do come in.'

Phillip followed him into the lounge. He had met Laurence Clare once before when he had come to value the property. He was tall and straight-backed and immaculately neat. Ex-forces; the stereotypical handle-bar moustache suggested RAF. Mrs Clare suffered from Alzheimer's disease and was now in permanent residential care. Her husband had decided that it was time to move.

'I shall miss this place, we've been very happy here, but it's isolated and I don't know how much longer I'll be able to drive. I need to move on before it's too late,' he explained. 'Can I get you some coffee?'

'Thank you, that would be nice.' Phillip sat down. While he waited he wondered if Clare had help to keep the place so spotless or whether his forces background enabled him to do so himself. The furnishings were on the fussy side but that might have reflected his wife's tastes.

Laurence Clare returned bearing a tray which he placed on the coffee table. He glanced at his watch and tutted before he began to pour. 'They're late.'

'I expect they'll be here in a minute, they might have got caught in traffic.' It was only a few minutes past ten thirty.

Clare raised an eyebrow as if to say, What traffic?

At eleven, after some slightly awkward conversation, Phillip rang Justin to see if he had received a message from the Abbotts.

'No, they haven't rung here. Perhaps they've broken down. Not everyone's got a mobile phone yet.'

'Thanks, Justin.' Phillip turned back to his client. 'No news, I'm afraid. I'm prepared to wait a little longer if that's all right with you.'

'Of course.'

They resumed their positions in the chairs they had previously chosen. Phillip felt uncomfortable and embarrassed. This sale was important, he didn't want his client to think him incompetent. Laurence Clare was obviously and understandably annoyed. He sat quietly, tapping the arms of his chair with his fingers. The man was quite capable of showing a couple around the house but that wasn't the way Phillip worked. He liked to add a personal touch to his business and he knew he was a good salesman. If a prospective buyer wasn't interested he could tell at once and didn't waste his time further but on the occasions when there was some hesitation he was able to lead them in the right direction.

'Do you suppose they're stupid enough to have got the wrong day?'

'It's possible, or perhaps some emergency has arisen. Excuse me a moment, I'll try their home number.' There was no reply. 'They're not in.' Phillip shrugged. It didn't mean they were on their way, though, the Abbotts might be anywhere.

'Well, we'd better forget it. It's almost twelve. I go to the Jolly Farmer for lunch before going on to visit my wife.' He stood up decisively. 'Let's hope the next lot of people will bother to show up.'

Phillip felt aggrieved, like a small child who has been chastised for someone else's misdemeanour. The man's tone of voice suggested it had somehow been Phillip's fault the Abbotts hadn't shown up.

The two men shook hands and walked to their cars. Phillip was furious with the Abbotts and hoped Clare didn't tell too many people what had happened. He drove back between the high hedges overgrown with wild flowers. Butterflies danced amongst them. The air smelled of summer; of the grasses which had seeded themselves in the hedges and spread, of ripening crops and the dust from dried mud. The hedges were lower once he left the winding country lanes, and spread all around him, now visible, was farmland. In the distance he could see the tower of the church at Little Endesley and beyond that the eaves of Mulberry Cottage.

Calmer for the peaceful drive, he told Justin about his wasted journey. After lunch one or two customers came in requiring details of houses they'd seen in the window and by the time Phillip set off for his afternoon appointment he had come to believe that the Abbotts had simply changed their minds but did not have the manners to inform him – either that or they'd decided they couldn't really afford the place.

When the same thing happened at Charleton Manor Phillip realized that they were still the targets for somebody's hatred. It was too much of a coincidence to be anything else.

'I do understand it isn't a crime,' he told DI Short who had driven out to his house in Little Endesley after Phillip's late afternoon telephone call. 'But I think it must have some bearing on all the other things which've been going on.'

Short was impressed with the house. But if an estate agent can't fix himself up with a decent pad, then who can? he asked himself. 'And you rang these people?'

'Yes. As soon as I got back to the office for the second time. There was still no reply from the Abbotts but Mrs Turner was at home. I got hold of Mr Abbott just before six when he got home from work. Their names and telephone numbers were genuine but the caller wasn't. Both parties told me the same thing, that they'd never heard of me or Little Endesley or the properties I mentioned. They seemed to think I was pulling some sort of scam. Obviously I wasn't but I was certainly made to look like a fool in the eyes of two of my clients.'

And word spreads. Short saw how damaging this could be to Hardy's business if someone made a habit of it. Anyone could have gone to a public library where all the telephone directories were available and picked out a couple of names and numbers at random. But why? 'Tell me how these appointments to view were made.'

'As you know, we advertise nationally. People see the adverts and ring us for details. Sometimes they don't even bother to do that. We don't skimp on our publicity, we use colour plates and give a good, clear description of the house and grounds. Quite often they'll simply make an appointment to view during the initial telephone call.'

'And you meet them at the house?'

'Sometimes. Sometimes they come to the office first. It all depends how far away from Little Endesley the place is.'

'How far did you have to travel today?'

'The Old Mill was just over half an hour's drive, Charleton Manor about fifty minutes, so it made sense to arrange to meet these so-called prospective buyers at the properties. Can I get you a drink, Inspector?'

'No, thanks.' Short sniffed before remembering he had a handkerchief in his pocket. He blew his nose and wondered if he was developing hay fever. The pollen count was high. 'From what you've told me it would seem that whoever led you on a wild goose chase either knows the area well or the way in which you work; probably both, in fact.'

Phillip got up and walked over to the window. There was a pile of bricks to his left which would form the new garage. The foundations had already been laid. Seeing them reminded him of all the bad things which had taken place and of something else he had forgotten until then. He turned to face Short, who was tugging at a trouser leg. 'Yes, I believe you're right. Certainly about knowing the area. We had another incident recently. A woman rang to say she wanted to put her barn conversion on the market. She gave detailed directions in order for us to find it and said she would wait for us there. Justin went over only to find a derelict shed. He made inquiries in the nearest village but no such address existed. He wasted most of a day.'

'A woman. And these appointments for today, were they made by a woman?'

'One was. I took the call. Justin took the other one. I'd have to ask him although I doubt if he'll remember. We seem to spend most of the day on the phone.'

'Any accent? Anything about her you can recall?'

'Yes. Mrs Abbott had a trace of a Midlands accent which, of course, is where she said she lives.'

'All right, Mr Hardy, we'll look into it but I don't think there's much we can do. If it wasn't for the other things we wouldn't be bothering at all. To trace the calls we'll need to know roughly when you received them. Do you keep any sort of record?'

Phillip shook his head. 'No, we just write the appointment in the diary along with the prospective buyer's telephone number in case the vendor postpones or cancels the appointment.' He smiled. 'Sorry, vendor's a little out of date now. I don't know why people have to keep changing perfectly suitable words.'

Neither did Short. Some of his vocabulary dated back five decades. 'If you can give me some approximate times we'll see what we can do.'

'The call I took was about three weeks ago. I'll have made a note of the date but not the time. I'll let you know if Justin can come up with anything.'

Short got up. It was almost seven, it had been a long day. Phillip walked him to his car. Birds were singing amongst the full summer foliage of the shrubs and bushes which lined the brick walls surrounding the house. It was a lovely evening but Phillip Hardy would not be able to enjoy it. He would be wondering what was going to happen next.

Driving back to Rickenham Green Short realized that tracing the hoax caller would be almost impossible. Any of Hardy's clients could have rung during the relevant periods and if they did pick up a mobile phone number used on the dates when the appointments had been made he would bet that it was no longer connected. He had advised Hardy to ring back anyone who wanted to view a property in future, to ensure they were genuine, although it was doubtful the same trick would be used again. Having been fooled twice on the same day Hardy was bound to be more careful.

I wonder if any of the other buggers are still in the pub, he thought. Because that was where he was heading.

My dearest Anna,

Perhaps you did not believe what I told you about your precious Phillip and Lorna but I can assure you it is absolutely true. You were both deceived, you and Robbie. What a nice little incestuous foursome you made.

Lorna is a dear friend of mine and she was desperately upset when Phillip mentioned ending the affair. It seemed he had met someone else.

How cruel of him that was after fucking her on a regular basis and leading her to imagine it would continue after hers and Robbie's marriage. She was, of course, only marrying him for his money.

Anyway, let me tell you what Lorna told me about the times she spent with Phillip. He had this thing about...

Anna threw the letter on the kitchen table as bile rose in her throat. Without thinking she had opened it, realizing too late her fingerprints would now be on it – not that it would matter much, the writer would have been just as careful the second time. It was vile and filthy. It was inconceivable that Phillip would do those things, things she didn't want to read but could not stop herself from looking at. How embarrassing to have to show it to the police, but show it she would. Something had to be done before they all lost their sanity. What sort of sick mind was doing this to her, to them all?

She drank a cup of tea before picking up the telephone. A few minutes wouldn't make any difference and she needed to gain control before making the call. Robbie had gone back to London and Phillip was at work but she would handle this alone.

Detective Sergeant Osborne arrived forty minutes later. Anna led her to the kitchen and gestured to the letter. 'It's worse than

215

the last one.'

Brenda leaned over and read it without touching it. Her hair, tied in a pony-tail, fell over her shoulder. She shoved it back impatiently. It wasn't just worse than the last one, it was revolting. She bagged it and placed the polythene holder in her shoulder-bag then turned to look at Anna who was visibly trembling. But she had to ask. 'Anna, do you think there is any grain of truth in these accusations?'

'No.' But she had hesitated for a fraction of a second. The doubts were setting in.

'Because, you see, it could have some bearing on why Lorna didn't turn up for the wedding and has now disappeared.'

'I understand the way you're thinking but I would swear to it that Phillip has been faithful to me.' She sat down suddenly as if her legs couldn't cope with the weight of her body. Please don't let it be true, she prayed.

Brenda nodded. Phillip had said the same thing himself. He had been shocked to find himself suspected of having an affair with his future stepson's future wife. 'Do you need someone to be with you?'

'No. I think I'd rather be alone. I don't feel like talking about this at the moment. I'll be fine, really.'

Back at the station Brenda expected Short to make a remark as vile as the words Anna Pearce had had to read but for once he

216

remained silent. 'This isn't going to stop until we catch someone,' Brenda said. 'I think–'

'Yes!'

They all turned to stare at Eddie Roberts who had punched the air as he yelled. 'It's Colorado. They're faxing us.'

They gathered around the machine as it churned out paper. There was no way the fax would be so long if they hadn't found Ottie Halmer. Eddie stood back to allow Ian to grab it and start reading. Minutes later he grinned.

'We've got her,' he said before giving them a precis of the information the Colorado police had sent.

At eight thirty Ian and Moira were sitting at their usual window table in the Taj Mahal with dishes of food between them on the hot-plates. Steam rose and, with it, the smell of garlic and spices. Ian poured some more wine and waited until Moira's chicken and peppers arrived on a sizzling dish before he served up his own food. They should have been celebrating, he had rung to book a table because the place was always busy on Fridays, but the day had not ended in quite the way he had hoped.

'You don't look terribly pleased with the results,' Moira said, noticing the frown on her husband's face.

'I really thought we'd have caught up with Lorna Daniels by now. We've had most of the day, or, rather, the Met have.' He chewed a piece of beef Madras and took a sip of wine. He'd rather have had beer but they didn't stock real ale and Moira always preferred wine.

'So what's gone wrong?'

'As you know, they found Ottie Halmer. From what we've learned it seems she's innocent in all this and the Colorado police said she was horrified at what's been going on. Anyway, the gist of it is this. Ottie Halmer was a very good friend of a woman called Paula Bowden. Paula was ill for years and finally died in January 2000. This was one of the reasons the Halmer woman decided to go for the job in the States, she no longer had any real ties in England. So she put her house on the market.'

'I can't see where this is going, Ian.'

'Then you'll have to be patient. Paula Bowden had a daughter, Rachel, who would now be about twenty-seven. The description she gave fits that of Lorna Daniels. Now here's where it gets interesting. Ottie, obviously knowing that Rachel's mother was dead, gave Rachel the keys to the house. She was returning to Germany to see her own mother and brother and to complete some work there before going to America. She's highly respected and well paid although she's got money in her own right as well. Rachel was to look after the house in her absence, to live there and to show people around if necessary. However, Ottie had returned and was living in the house again when the Baxters came and made their offer so they didn't ever meet Rachel.

'Robbie Pearce wasn't lying when he said he'd been to the house many times, except he believed that Lorna, as he knew her to be, owned it.'

'What about her own place? Rachel's?'

'She'd sold the flat she'd lived in with her mother and was renting until she found somewhere to buy that she really liked. When Ottie Halmer made her proposal almost a year later it was an ideal situation for her. She gave up the rented flat because living rent-free in Miss Halmer's house gave her a chance to add to the money she'd made from the sale of her mother's place.'

'Okay, I can see all that even if you didn't explain it very clearly, but you told me Robbie said they met by chance so if Lorna Daniels or Rachel, whatever she's called, is the person causing all this havoc what motive could she possibly have?'

'Your guess is as good as mine. We do now know that it was true that Lorna, sorry, Rachel was illegitimate and an only child and that her mother died, although not in a car accident. Miss Halmer confirmed that much. The question is, who was her father? Ottie never met him but it wasn't true he deserted Paula Bowden when her daughter was a baby. He was often at the flat and Paula talked about him quite openly. There was some secret, Ottie was aware of that but she didn't pry. Then, about three or four years before Paula died the bloke did actually disappear. Paula never heard from him again and the payments he had been giving her ceased. All we know is that his name was John. Ottie always assumed that his surname was Bowden and that Paula and Rachel had taken his name.

'Ottie also said that Paula lived a pretty reclusive life, only seeming to need John and Rachel. When John disappeared she turned more and more to Ottie which was why she felt she couldn't abandon her, nor her daughter completely after Paula died.'

'People really do have a habit of disappearing recently. So now you have the girl's real name why can't she be found?'

'For one thing it's the school holidays. Yes, we'd already checked with the school where Lorna was supposed to be teaching but we'd drawn a blank. This time we discovered that she did work there under the name of Bowden but only until the months before her mother's death when she took compassionate leave to look after her. She didn't go back, she got another teaching job in north

London. She hasn't given in her notice at this latest school so it's assumed she'll return there next term.

'We also spoke to Frankie Holland, the second woman whose address Rachel used. And guess what?'

Moira shook her head. 'No, hold on, I think I can. Does she have children?'

'That's it. Two of them. One's a toddler but Matthew's five and has been at school a year. No need to tell you the name of his teacher.'

'So Rachel just looked up her address in the files and decided to use it for her own while she played whatever game she's playing?'

'I don't think it worked that way. The records would be locked up in the secretary's room or inaccessible to other staff on the computer. But Frankie Holland told us that Rachel had taken Matthew home once when he'd become ill during the lunch hour. They'd contacted Frankie but she doesn't have a car and it was snowing. The school decided that it was easier for a member of staff to run him home than to drag his mother and baby out into the cold and to risk Matthew's condition worsening. Rachel would have seen it was an ideal sort of address to use for someone in her position.'

'And the school has given you her present address?'

'Not yet. The only two people who have keys to the personnel files are either out or away and by the time we got through all this other stuff it was too late to contact the people at the records office.'

'Records office?'

'Where every teacher is listed.'

'And tomorrow's Saturday.'

'Precisely. Are you leaving that?' Ian gestured towards some pieces of chicken with his fork.

'Yes. I'm full. You have it.'

He scraped it on to his plate. 'All we can hope is that one or other of the keyholders is at home tonight or in the morning.'

Moira sat back and sipped some wine. 'What about the electoral roll?'

'We tried that. She isn't on it, not under the name of Rachel Bowden or Lorna Daniels. However, if she's been moving around it might be that she hasn't yet had a form sent to her at the new address. The last record was for the time when she lived at the flat with her mother.'

'There you are, then, the father's name should be there too.'

'It isn't. He was away a lot, he probably had another address.'

'What does he do?'

'Ottie didn't seem to know. A businessman was all she could tell them. Do you want coffee?'

'No, thanks. I've just about room to finish my wine. I take it this means you'll be going in tomorrow.' It was a statement rather than a question.

'No. They can reach me at home or on the mobile if necessary. Have you heard anything from Mark and Yvette?'

'Nothing at all. But you know what they're like. They'll ring at the last minute to say they're in England.' It was an annoying habit but it didn't stop Moira from longing to see her only child again.

Ian asked for the bill then ate both of the mint chocolates which came with it on the plate. 'Ready?' he said when he'd pocketed his credit card. 'I need the walk after that lot.'

'Well, you didn't have to eat what I left as well.'

'You know me, I can't see food wasted.'

Unless it's salad, Moira thought as they walked back through the busy streets towards Belmont Terrace.

Chapter Fifteen

Inspector Short had no real objection to being at work on a Saturday. For one thing he would claim the time back, secondly he had no family ties and thirdly he had no interest in sport, certainly not cricket.

'You should try it. We take a picnic and a bottle of wine and sit on the grass in the sun,' Brenda had told him the previous day when he'd asked how she was spending the weekend. She and Andrew would be on their way now to whichever cow-patted field the local match was taking place on. And when the Chief and Alan Campbell got on to football he felt like puking. In fact he wasn't far off it now although for different reasons.

He had made it to the pub to find only Greg Grant remaining. Greg had imagined himself safe because Short was elsewhere when Ian suggested a quick drink before he met Moira. Greg had stayed for one more then wisely gone home. At eight, Short had walked down the High Street and purchased a bottle of champagne, the cheapest the off-licence had to offer, and a takeaway Chinese for two. These items he took to Nancy's place because she was expecting him. Ian's meal out with Moira was for celebratory purposes; they had traced Ottie Halmer and would soon find Lorna Daniels. The champagne was not. To Short the job was just a job, cases were solved or they weren't. He never got depressed or excited like the others. Despite his single state, despite the relative squalor of his small box of a house, John Short had a life outside work. He had Nancy, as and when the mood suited either of them, although the relationship was not exclusive. They both liked their fun. And videos. He was addicted to films, especially when he could watch them at home with a beer in his hand and the freedom to belch and fart at will, both of which he frequently did because of his unhealthy diet. There were drinks with the lads, and the ladette, he amended as he thought of the luscious Brenda, and drinks with friends who were nothing to do with the police. No, the champagne had been for Nancy simply because it was her favourite tipple. He preferred beer or whisky.

They had eaten and drunk. Then things had gone wrong. Lying between sheets which smelled of perfume and the musk of Nancy's body, he had been enjoying one of his best-loved sights, watching her undress, slowly revealing the folds of her flesh, her hennaed hair half hiding her breasts as she bent to unfasten her stockings. She had never worn tights. That was when he had felt it, that first watery gurgle, the warning of what was to come. He hadn't drunk much, only a few beers. It had to be the Chinese. And there was only one toilet. They had spent the night sharing it.

Now he felt marginally better but not good enough to do more than sit at his desk and wait for the telephone to ring. Someone had to be there in case the Met had any information relating to Rachel Bowden. A detective from another team could have handled it but they had agreed that they wanted to deal with this themselves. What was happening to the Pearces was baffling them all.

Short was on his second digestive which he dunked into milky coffee when the handset nearest to him rang. It made him jump. 'Sod it,' he said as the soggy half of the biscuit dropped into his mug. 'Detective Inspector Short,' he snapped as if it was the caller's fault he had lost both biscuit and coffee.

'Good morning, sir. Sergeant Greenaway, Met Police. It's about Rachel Bowden.'

Smooth bugger, Short thought, mistaking the exaggerated politeness for the real thing. 'Have you found her?'

'Not as such. But we've got the address from the school secretary. We caught her at home this morning. We then called at Miss Bowden's house. She wasn't in but a neighbour confirmed she'd gone away for a few days.' Greenaway talked for a few more minutes.

'Bugger it. And no one knows where she's gone. Don't tell me.' There was no response. Short realized he was being taken literally. 'Go on, do tell me. I take it I'm right, Sergeant Greenaway?'

'You are, sir. Do you want us to keep on trying or will your own men carry on?'

'We'll leave it with you, if that's all right. No point in having people down there indefinitely. She might be gone for ages. Thanks for your help, by the way.'

'No problem. I'll give you the address.'

Short wrote it down then rang Ian to bring him up to date. There didn't seem much point in hanging around any longer. He decided to treat himself to a browse around the video shop and forgo his usual Saturday lunchtime in the pub.

Robbie Pearce was trying to put his life back together. On Saturday morning he stowed Lorna's suitcase in the boot of the car then drove around until he'd found a skip where he dumped it. Returning to the flat he removed every trace of her; a half-used lipstick in the bathroom cabinet, a pair of ear-rings, some cheap sunglasses and the herbal teabags she occasionally fancied.

Feeling as if he had actually achieved something, he stood in the window and watched people enjoying the sunshine. He needed to get out. The flat was depressing now. He'd sell it if his mother didn't object. She had insisted that he keep the deeds, which had been transferred to his name before the wedding. Anna had intended handing them over on the day as her gift. Instead she had given them to him on the Sunday morning when he was at Mulberry Cottage. All the other gifts had been returned.

Robbie rang a couple of friends and found one who was free for a game of tennis. Some strenuous exercise would do him good, help rid him of the tension in his shoulders and some of the anger which was building up inside him.

He won the match but took little pleasure in doing so. Showering the sweat from his body he realized that Lorna had deprived him of what he most needed now: friends, real friends. He had made the mistake so many people make; after meeting her he had loosened his ties with some of his old friends and lost touch with others completely. He had not been aware of how she was manipulating him by claiming she wanted to be with him every possible minute. And now Malcolm, the man he had beaten by three sets to two, had to rush off to meet his girlfriend. Weekends would be the worst times, he saw that now. Many people he knew were married, as he should have been, and some had children and family commitments. As the years passed it would be harder to make new friends.

He went home to the empty flat and an evening of television or reading after he'd had something to eat, a meal which would be eaten alone and without enjoyment.

Snap out of it, you stupid bastard, he told himself. Self-pity won't get you anywhere. It was a failing he abhorred, but he saw how easily it could overtake you.

When the telephone rang he assumed it would be his mother and hoped that nothing else had gone wrong. She had told him about the disgusting second letter and Phillip's non-existent purchasers.

'Ah, Robbie, I'm glad I found you in. I tried several times earlier.'

'James?' His boss had never rung him at the weekend, had never rung him at home, in fact.

'There's something we need to discuss and I didn't want to bring it up at work.'

'Go ahead.' Robbie was puzzled but perhaps there was another security alert. Since it was discovered that terrorists laundered money and then deposited it in the most respectable of places the bank had

had to be very careful.

'Not over the telephone.'

'Monday morning, then? I can cancel my meeting.'

'No. Can you manage this evening?'

This had to be very serious. 'Yes. Yes, of course I can. Where and what time?'

'Would it be possible for me to come to your flat?'

Robbie said it would and waited for his arrival. He assumed James would travel by tube or taxi so got out bottles and glasses.

'I'll have a gin and tonic, please,' James said when Robbie had shown him in and asked what he wanted to drink.

The sun had moved over the roofs of the buildings opposite and the room was now in shadow. James sat down and crossed his legs before taking a sip of his drink. The bubbles of tonic fizzed in the glass as they rose to the surface. He listened to the sounds of the building as he tried to think how best to phrase what he had to say. Pipes gurgled faintly as someone above emptied a bath, the lift in the hallway outside whined and muted voices could be heard as a couple passed the doorway. He decided to come straight to the point. 'Yesterday, just before I left the office, I received a telephone call. The caller chose to remain anonymous, which I took as a sign that there was no truth in what followed, I hope I'm right.'

Robbie felt himself tense further. This was not about terrorism, this was personal and he had a good idea what was coming next. 'A telephone call? About what?'

'I was advised to look into your client portfolio to see if there were any, ah, any inaccuracies.'

'You mean I was being accused of fiddling the books. Of fraud. That's what you're trying to say, isn't it, James?' He looked at the man he had thought he knew, a man who looked and dressed like the city banker he was: urbane, unostentatious, smooth grey hair and plain glasses. And now with a face which was grimmer than he'd ever seen it.

'If you must put it like that, then, yes. I didn't detain you last night because I needed time to think.'

'And to check, no doubt.' There was bitterness and anger in his tone.

'No, Robbie, I didn't do that. I wanted to speak to you first. If, there are any discrepancies I wanted to give you the chance to admit to them.'

'My God, what do you take me for?' He gulped some gin. 'I have never done anything dishonest in my life – and I never shall. Why should I need to? I've got everything I want. I own this flat outright and I can hardly complain about my salary.'

'But not quite everything, Robbie. You see,

that's why I wanted to talk to you. I thought, perhaps, the strain of the last few weeks ... well, you know...' He left the sentence unfinished. Obviously Robbie knew.

Robbie exhaled deeply to release some of the tension. Anger was useless, he could see James's point of view. He believed he'd cracked up after losing Lorna then his grandmother. 'Go ahead and check, call in the auditors, even the police if you wish, but you won't find anything amiss.' He hoped he was right, he hoped whoever was ruining his life had not somehow managed to gain access to his files. 'Look, there's something I want to tell you, something that might explain why you got that call.' He gave a detailed account of events starting from his wedding day. James listened without interrupting. When he had finished Robbie refilled their glasses. 'Now do you believe me? Or do you think it's even more reason for me to have turned to crime?'

'I believe you. But, Robbie, I still have to check. In my position I really can't afford to ignore what was said even though I don't believe it. Don't worry. I'll do it personally on Monday. You take the day off. I'd rather not go through your files with you watching. I feel bad enough as it is.'

'Why not tomorrow?'

James looked uncomfortable. 'My wife and I are visiting friends tomorrow.'

While my job, my future hangs in the balance. Well, thank you very much, James Attwood, Robbie thought. 'And when you do discover I'm innocent I feel you owe it to me to tell the police in Rickenham Green about this anonymous telephone call.'

'Certainly I will.' He stood and handed Robbie his glass. 'No hard feelings?'

Robbie shook his head but he knew how it would be. Others would notice his absence and however careful James was he would not be able to conceal the fact that he was checking Robbie's files. And they would put two and two together and come up with the wrong answer. And mud sticks. Begrudgingly, he shook hands and showed James out. Another compartment of his life had been touched and ruined. The easy companionship that had existed between James and himself would cease to be.

Robbie shut the door. He was no longer hungry. He felt used up, tired and defeated. There was nothing to be done until Monday. If he still had his job then he would take stock and get back out in the world. Perhaps, one day, he might even meet another woman he could love.

A chilly wind blew clouds quickly across the sky. Their large shadows swept over the streets and buildings of Rickenham Green and sent litter scuttling in irritable bursts.

The change of weather had taken some people by surprise and they were unsuitably dressed for the drop in the temperature. Not so Inspector Short, who wore a suit winter or summer, quite often the same one, but it was he who gained from other people's lack of foresight. By other people's he meant the distaff side of the human race. The hems of dresses were lifted to expose bare thighs and nipples stood out beneath skimpy tops. One young woman wore a skirt so short that the ends of her long, blonde hair almost hid it when they weren't being flung around her shoulders.

With his hands in his pockets Short stopped to stare at her retreating back, uncaring that people were watching him. I could spare that one an hour or two of my time, he thought as he crossed the road to the sandwich bar to purchase his mid-morning fix of cholesterol.

Ian was in the general office taking a call when he returned. There was still no news of Rachel Bowden but they weren't too concerned. Thank goodness milkmen still existed, and not everyone relied on supermarkets. The man who delivered milk in Rachel's street had told the local police that she would be back on Wednesday, that she had only cancelled her milk for a week.

'That was a man called James Attwood. He's Robbie Pearce's boss,' Ian told Short before explaining about the accusation and wondering aloud why Robbie Pearce hadn't told them himself. 'If there is any truth in it it puts a different complexion on things.' But he couldn't see young Pearce as an embezzler however hard he tried.

Short whistled through his teeth as he placed the bag containing doughnuts on his desk. 'That's a pretty serious charge. And I bet Attwood's thinking there's no smoke without fire.'

Brenda studied her nails and hoped to be spared more clichés.

'Was the call from a woman?'

'Yes. Unfortunately it came through the main switchboard which will make it harder to trace – the bank receives literally hundreds of calls every day and Attwood can't remember exactly what time this one was. Late afternoon was as near as he could get.'

'It's got to be her. Rachel Bowden.' Alan Campbell was thinking aloud. 'Whoever we talk to tells us they were contacted by a woman.'

'Well, hopefully we'll know by Wednesday. There will be people in place ready to pick her up from first thing on Wednesday morning.' And when we've got her perhaps we'll find out what's really been going on, Ian thought as he reached into his shirt pocket for his cigarettes.

But it was sooner than that that their luck began to change.

Robbie had not been up long when the doorbell rang. It was only seven thirty but perhaps the postman had a package for him. Confusion and astonishment rendered him speechless when he opened the door, and then he smiled, happy again, almost ecstatic. 'Lorna. Oh, God, you don't know what I've been going through. Come in, tell me what happened. We've all been worried sick. Why on earth did you change your mind?' He was gabbling but he couldn't help it.

She followed him into the lounge. Whatever had happened to her over the past couple of weeks, she remained very beautiful. He offered her coffee which she refused. He wanted to touch her, to kiss her, to hear her say it was all a mistake, nothing more than last-minute nerves. But she sat there looking calm and in control, cold even, and then he remembered how she had lied to him.

'There are things I have to tell you and when you've heard them you will never see me again.' Her voice was harsh, not at all as he remembered it. 'I want you to listen very carefully, Robbie, I want you to understand what your family's done to me. And not just me.'

She spoke at length and with each sentence Robbie felt reality slipping away from him. Her words had changed his life for ever. 'Haven't you done enough damage?' he finally managed to ask. 'Why have you come back just to tell more lies?' But she wasn't lying, he knew that really. Everything she said rang true and, in retrospect, it made certain things fall into place.

She smiled, then got up and walked towards where he was sitting. 'How about a kiss for old times' sake?'

He stared at her in amazement that she could suggest such a thing. And then, as she stood immediately in front of his chair and he could smell her familiar perfume, he saw the knife she pulled from her bag and understood that being seated put him at an awful disadvantage.

'We've got her, sir.' Eddie Roberts' hair stood on end because he had been running his fingers through it excitedly. 'She went to Pearce's flat. He called the police and an ambulance.'

Only Ian and Brenda were present. Short was in another room, on the telephone to the headmistress of the school where Rachel taught, although that call was now redundant. The rest of the team were catching up on other cases or out interviewing witnesses.

'I think you can make yourself clearer than

that,' Ian commented drily.

'She went to the flat early this morning. Pearce let her in and she stabbed him. He managed to restrain her before she repeated the exercise. Knocked her out cold, in fact. I don't suppose he had much choice.'

'Is he badly hurt?' Brenda asked.

'No one knows yet. Bowden's in a holding cell. When the police surgeon's given her the once-over we can go down there and collect her.'

'Whatever she's got to say about everything else at least this charge will stick. Are they ringing us to let us know when she's ours?'

'Yes. But they haven't contacted Mrs Pearce, they assumed we'd rather send someone along in person.'

Ian felt a great sense of relief. This ought to be an end to it, and the Pearces could get on with their lives. He looked across at Brenda. She had some sort of rapport with Anna Pearce, but first he needed to know if the hospital had informed Robbie's mother of his injuries. 'Ring the hospital, Eddie, see if they're any wiser as to his condition and ask if they've told Mrs Pearce.'

'No news yet, he's still in theatre. They said to ring back in a couple of hours. And they assumed the police had done the necessary,' Eddie said when he'd finished the call.

'Thanks. Brenda?'

She nodded, knowing exactly what the Chief expected of her. Brenda picked up her jacket and the large shoulderbag which went almost everywhere with her and left.

Anna had been about to go over to her mother's place to begin sorting things out for the charity shop when she saw the car turning into the drive. She recognized the driver and guessed it could only be more bad news. The policewoman got out. Her face gave nothing away but the fact that she was not smiling did. It was with a feeling of resignation that Anna went to answer the door.

'I'm sure you want to set off for London immediately,' Brenda said when she had broken the news and given Anna time to absorb it. On top of everything else it can't have been easy.

'Yes. I can't not be there.' Anna's reactions had been mixed. She had felt a surge of maternal love and protectiveness towards her son and hatred for the girl who had hurt him both mentally and physically, but there was also a sense of relief. 'It'll stop now, won't it,' she said with certainty. 'Lorna's got to be behind it all, although God knows why after the way in which we treated her.'

Brenda did not know the answer. 'Is there someone who can drive you?' she asked instead.

'I'm sure Phillip will. If not I'll be quite all right on my own.'

Brenda thought she probably would be. She looked calm now that she believed it really was all over. Soon they would all know one way or another.

Satisfied that Phillip Hardy had agreed to call for Anna immediately, Brenda drove back to the station.

By five fifteen that evening Rachel Bowden was sitting in a stuffy interview room while Brenda and Chief Inspector Roper listened in disbelief. It had happened before and it would happen again, but what amazed them was how long someone could actually get away with it.

Chapter Sixteen

She was stunning, there was no doubt about that. Even Brenda recognized the effect she would have on men. Rachel Bowden, whom they had known for so long as Lorna Daniels, was of average height and slender with feminine curves. Her clear skin radiated health and her eyes, slightly slanted upwards at the corners, were a deep brown. Her mouth was wide and soft and when she spoke her lips revealed perfect teeth. No wonder Robbie Pearce was so desperate to find her.

Rachel listened as Ian explained the interview procedure She had refused the offer of a solicitor. Her attitude suggested that she didn't care what happened to her now.

Where to start? Ian thought. With today, I'll work back from the end. 'Why did you stab Robbie Pearce, the man you were supposed to marry?'

'Because I hated him. I hated him and his whole family for what they'd done to me and to my mother. She died because of them.'

'Our understanding is that she was ill and had been so for many years and that her death was only a matter of time.'

'Yes, she was ill, but after my father left without saying a word her condition deteriorated. She adored him, lived for him really. I thought she felt the same way about me. I had no idea she was living a lie.'

'I think it might be best if you tell us what happened rather than my asking you questions. Is that all right with you?' Ian was lost already.

She nodded then took a deep breath. 'Just before my mother died she told me that my father was married, that he had another family and that when he left her she assumed he was tired of his double life and had gone back to them permanently. She never got over this. Oh–' She smiled. 'Of course, you don't know, do you? John Pearce, Robbie's father, was also my father. Now you see why I could never have married Robbie. We had sex, there was no way out of that, it was part of the plan.

'I knew that my father was away on business a lot but it was only two years ago that I learned the reason for all his other absences. My mother always told me he was an atheist, more than that, that he hated any and all forms of religion. This, I was brought up to believe, was why he was never around at Christmas and Easter. He was supp-osedly travelling and studying various forms of art. He wasn't, of course, he was with that bitch Anna. I wanted to destroy them all.'

'Did you set fire to Phillip Hardy's garage?' Ian needed something factual to grasp while the enormity of what he'd been told sank in.

'Yes. I thought the house would burn with it. I thought after I didn't turn up for the wedding the cosy little threesome would all be at Anna's house. And before you ask, I also sent Anna those letters. I wanted to destroy their relationship, just like I wanted to destroy Phillip's business. And more than anything I wanted to kill Robbie. He had what should have been mine. I almost succeeded.'

'What about Audrey Field, Robbie's grandmother.'

Rachel sniffed. 'Another smug one. Her daughter had a happy first marriage and now she was thrilled she'd found someone new. I wanted to frighten the old bat so she'd move in with Anna. That would've been the final straw. It would put even more pressure on Anna and Phillip's relationship.'

'Audrey Field is dead.'

'What?'

Rachel's eyes were wide. She hadn't known, she hadn't meant for it to happen. Ian found it odd that it should upset her when she had intended to kill another person.

'How did she die?'

He told her. 'How did you arrange that

little piece of nastiness?'

'Robbie and Phillip told me all about Rickenham Green. I knew I'd find someone in the Black Horse who was willing to do me a favour in return for payment. It wasn't difficult. I only went in there twice. I overheard a conversation and knew I'd found the man I needed. Audrey would've been unsettled after those phone calls, he was to break in and tie her up. No more than that. Oh, except for taking a few bits to make it look like burglary.'

So she had been responsible for it all. A well-thought-out campaign which had fortunately now come to an end. 'You met Robbie in an art gallery. How did that come about?' It couldn't have been by chance. Ian realized Rachel Bowden had been planning her moves for some time before she acted.

Moira was dressmaking when Ian got home. It was a hobby she took up and dropped at will. With a couple of pins held firmly between her lips she looked up when Ian found her in the dining-room and smiled as best she could. She placed the pins back in their box and switched off the sewing-machine.

Ian kissed the top of her head and asked if she wanted tea or something stronger.

'The latter, please. I haven't had one yet, I thought I'd wait for you.' Ian had rung to say he'd be late, and why. She knew he would want to discuss the case before he ate so she hadn't yet eaten either. She understood his need to talk, it helped to clarify things in his mind so that he could spot any mistakes they might have made. His total trust in her was only a part of what he felt for her and she was fully aware of that. The dress would have to wait. She followed him to the kitchen where the last of the sunshine slanted through the windows, reminding her they needed a clean. Plants were swaying in the strengthening wind. Moira shivered. 'You'd think summer was over the way the weather's changed. I was almost tempted to put the heating on tonight.'

'It's certainly fresher.' Ian handed her a glass of wine. 'Something smells nice.'

'Moussaka. Home-made. What a fiddle. At least I made enough to freeze some.' As if he'd be interested, she thought. But then, he still recounted every move in football games he'd gone to watch even though she knew nothing about the game and had no intention of learning. Marriage was like that. 'So the elusive Rachel Bowden has turned up?'

Ian joined her at the kitchen table, a glass of beer in front of him. 'Indeed she has. Turned up and we've turned over a few stones under which nasty things lay.'

'Oh?' Moira saw that he was going to

enjoy telling this. She took a sip of her wine. 'Go on then.'

'It's hard to know where to start. A lot of what she told Robbie was the truth, if doctored a little. She was illegitimate, an only child, and lived with her mother in London, and her mother did die two years back, but not in a car crash. She's admitted that everything that was done to the Pearces and Phillip Hardy was down to her. She hated them all with a vengeance.'

'Why?'

'I'll come to that. Do you remember me telling you about the stabbing outside the Black Horse?' Moira nodded. 'Well, Dave Johnson, the man who was injured, had been approached by Rachel the previous night. She'd heard him speaking to someone and knew he was her man. Then he was joined by Dennis Suitor but she didn't want to miss her chance.'

'She wanted him to stab Suitor? You told me Suitor had taken the knife off Johnson, obviously it all went wrong. But why would she want him to do that?'

'You've got it wrong. She wanted Dave Johnson to scare the living daylights out of Audrey Field so she would move in with Anna.' He explained Rachel Bowden's objectives and the reasons for writing the letters. 'She was convinced Anna would not let her mother live on her own any longer.'

'That doesn't explain why Dave Johnson got injured.'

'We've arrested him. I think he was sort of glad in a way. He had no idea Audrey would die. Well, he admitted that both he and Suitor were drunk and that Suitor didn't usually drink that much. He told him what he was about to do just as they were leaving the pub. Suitor, it seems, went berserk and told him he was despicable. We've questioned him again now. He still can't really recall what he did but he said he imagined that was probably his reason for pulling the knife from Johnson's pocket... Another drink? I'm having one.'

'No, I'm fine for the moment, thanks.'

Ian got up and poured more beer. 'To lubricate the throat,' he said with a grin. 'Back to Rachel Bowden. She was the one who rang Robbie's boss and she also arranged those bogus house viewings with Hardy. It's easier to disguise your voice over a telephone. She wanted to cause strife in every part of their lives. She wanted Robbie to suffer even further before she killed him which, she admitted, was her intention all along. I imagine our tame shrink will conclude that her discovery and the death of her mother coming so quickly after it will have sent her over the top. It was an obsession and now it's over and she doesn't seem to care about anything.

'Anyway, she went to his flat this morning and tried to kill him. Thank goodness he was able to overcome her and call for help.'

'My God, Ian, that's awful. Whatever made the girl so unstable?'

'She'd discovered her father was John Pearce, Robbie's father.' His words had the desired effect. Moira's jaw dropped. 'Yes, he got away with it for all those years. But Rachel knew nothing of this until the day before her mother died. Paula Bowden thought Rachel had a right to know about her half-brother, maybe she even fancied that this other half of the family would look after her daughter.'

Moira said nothing while she thought about it. 'If she didn't know about Robbie, how did she meet him and the rest of them?'

'I'll come to that. Rachel's mother died a bitter and disappointed woman. She told Rachel that she had always known there had never been any chance of her and John living together on a permanent basis, and she accepted that. What got to her was the fact that John disappeared just at the time that her health was declining. She had no way of knowing that he had died. Neither did Rachel until she tried to find her father.'

'Couldn't she simply have rung his place of work? And surely he had a mobile.'

'No. He didn't have a place of work. He travelled around valuing paintings, et cetera.

Work came from all quarters and the arrangements were made over the phone. For a while Paula did try ringing his mobile but she finally realized it was no longer connected to a network. She couldn't write either because she didn't know his Suffolk address. Besides, she had made a vow not to do anything which might harm his marriage and, according to Rachel, she knew nothing of the existence of his London flat or she might've written there.'

'Hang on, are you telling me he was keeping three places going?'

'Precisely.'

'I still don't see how he got away with it. All right, he travelled a lot, he could use that excuse to both women, but what about holidays?'

Ian told her about John Pearce's supposed aversion to religion. 'He managed to share himself around fairly evenly. When he was with Anna he knew Paula would not dream of contacting him, and we assume that when he was with Paula, Anna got hold of him on his mobile. There was no landline at his flat in those days, that way his legal family couldn't check on his presence there. He'd thought it out very carefully, no doubt his daughter takes after him in that respect.

'He'd only been married a short time when he met Paula. Anna was going through an awkward pregnancy. We'll never know if he meant to end the affair once Robbie was born but it seems unlikely in that it continued until his death. Paula became pregnant almost instantly. Perhaps he felt he couldn't dump her then, and later, when he found out about her illness, didn't have the heart to and felt duty bound to stay.'

'Maybe he really loved her. It's possible, you know, to love two people at once, usually for different reasons.'

'Is it?' Ian frowned and hoped that Moira was not speaking from experience. Just the thought of it made him feel sick.

'Go on then, how did Rachel discover her half-brother?'

'As hard as this is to believe, Rachel assumed her father's name was Bowden. No one ever came to the flat when he was there, Paula had very few friends. This was deliberate because of the life she had chosen to lead. If they went out together they got a baby-sitter. When Rachel was older she had her own friends but because of her mother's illness rarely invited them home. If the three of them went out together it was never locally so she'd never heard him addressed by his real name. Only when she learned of John Pearce's double life did she realize how abnormal things were.'

'But if you grow up with them you believe it is the norm.'

'True.'

'What about the TV appearances? Surely she'd have watched them?'

'No. She knew nothing about them. But Rachel did tell us that on several occasions, even when she thought her mother wasn't up to it, she'd insisted on going to the cinema. Rachel accompanied her.

'Anyway, after her mother died she went to pieces. They had been so very close. Now she'd discovered she'd been deceived by both parents and she couldn't forgive John for having a proper family and a house and all the trimmings in the country, even though she and Paula had always been well provided for until his death. It was John she set out to get. She spent weeks going around the art galleries but they didn't all use his services. Finally someone told her he was dead and had been for some time. She was furious. It was probably this which sent her right over the top. She couldn't get to him now or ever, and no one was prepared to give her the address of the house where he'd lived with his wife. In the end she started by going through all the London telephone directories. Paula had told Rachel that she and Robbie were almost the same age, that when John disappeared he had just finished at university. This gave her the idea, though God knows why, that Robbie might have gravitated to London. She tried every R. Pearce in the book.'

'She sounds totally obsessional.'

'She is, you can take it from me. And she shows absolutely no remorse. She didn't have to look far. It didn't take many calls before she was rewarded with a man who answered and said, yes, he was Robbie James Pearce and his father's name was John. Before he could ask her why she was ringing she hung up. Naturally, his address was in the phone book. To make sure, she went to the flat and watched him.'

'How would she recognize him?'

'She didn't know but she'd decided to think of ways in which she could get talking to him if all else failed. Of course, once she saw him there was no question he was John's son. She said it was like looking at her father as a younger man. From there it was simple. She followed him to the gallery one night and talked her way in. Don't ask me how, but if you saw her you'd see why that was possible.'

'Oh, good-looking, is she?'

'An absolute stunner.'

Moira got up to lower the heat of the oven. She had planned to eat about now but saw that there was much more to come. A salad was waiting in a bowl in the fridge.

'Rachel set out to make Robbie fall in love with her. Her looks were an instant advantage and she made herself become exactly what she saw he wanted in a woman. Anna

Pearce said how much Rachel enjoyed planning the wedding. I bet she did, knowing what it would do to Robbie when she didn't turn up. Once she knew enough about the family, things took off from there. And there was the added bonus of Ottie Halmer asking her to house-sit.'

'But why use a false name and use false addresses?'

'The name Bowden would mean nothing to Robbie but she didn't want him to find her afterwards nor did she want to be caught by us. Had Ottie not made the offer she intended telling Robbie that she shared a room with another girl and couldn't take him back there. Whether he'd have believed her is another matter. He would have known that, as a teacher, she'd be able to afford something a little better than what she intended describing.'

'And Anna never suspected anything was wrong?'

'It seems unlikely. She had a nice life, a busy life, and a son who was doing well, and her mother and plenty of friends living nearby. Nothing had changed, you see, it had been the same throughout their marriage. Presumably he didn't mess around elsewhere and, if you're right, presumably he was a loving husband.'

'You said it seems unlikely, about Anna knowing. Don't you know?'

Ian shook his head. 'Robbie knows because Rachel told him this morning. Anna's with Robbie now. We haven't had a chance to talk to her because she left for London before we interviewed Rachel. Whether Robbie tells her is up to him.'

'You mean you aren't going to tell her?'

Ian met her eyes. 'Like I said, she might already know. I've been thinking hard about this. She's suffered so much already it would only cause more pain.'

'And a rift between her and Robbie if he decides not to say anything.'

'Yes, that's possible. Except I'm sure Anna will ask. She knows we've arrested Rachel, she's bound to want to know why she did all those things. In which case we'll certainly have to tell her.'

'Will Robbie be all right?'

'Yes, eventually. He'll be in hospital for a while yet, though. There was considerable internal damage.'

'And Rachel? Psychiatric reports, I suppose, treatment instead of prison? Yet she planned it all so very carefully.'

'Mental illness doesn't signify lack of intelligence. I'm shattered, Moira, I think I'll have a quick shower before we eat. Is that all right with you?'

'Yes, that's fine. Go ahead.' Moira thought about it. The death of a mother who was only in her fifties and the revelations which preceded it would be enough to send anyone over the top. But to want to kill the innocent people involved was unthinkable. Moira wondered how she would have reacted and guessed that her desire might be to want to meet the other family, partly out of curiosity, partly to try to discover why her father had felt the need of a second one.

'You're thoughtful,' Ian said when he reappeared more casually dressed, his hair still wet from the shower.

'She went to an awful lot of trouble.'

'Who? Rachel Bowden?'

'Yes. But to sleep with a man you know is your half-brother, I can't understand that.'

'I suppose if you feel your cause is strong enough you'll do anything. I would guess that not only did she want to break his heart, to coin a phrase, but she also wanted to disgust him when she finally told him the truth.'

'In which case Robbie might decide not to tell his mother. It would mean admitting his part in incest even if he was unaware that that was what it was.'

'I see your point, love and I'll bear it in mind.' He picked up the paper, indicating to Moira that he'd had enough of work. She put the plates on the table and took the steaming moussaka out of the oven, praying that if she did find out, the news wouldn't destroy Anna Pearce further.

Chapter Seventeen

After ten days Robbie Pearce was considered well enough to be discharged from hospital but he would not be returning to work for several weeks. DCI Roper had spoken to James Attwood and explained the situation, which meant Robbie would be able to return to his job with a clean reputation. For the time being he was staying with his mother in Mulberry Cottage.

Anna's relief that her son was recovering and his attacker under arrest was profound. They must now try to put all that behind them. But it was Robbie's state of mind which worried her now. He hardly spoke except to answer questions and she had to persuade him to leave the house, to breathe some fresh air now and again. He seemed to be sinking further and further into a deep depression and she suspected it was not entirely to do with the painful wedding day or his grandmother's death. When she asked what was troubling him he denied anything being wrong. There seemed to be nothing she could do.

At the end of his first week at home she carried a tray of tea out to the sunbed on which he was lying. The book at his side lay unopened. She noticed the first hint of autumn in the leaves of the trees, a faint yellowing amongst the greens. In four months' time Christmas would be upon them, a Christmas which would be so very different from the previous one when Audrey and the girl they had known as Lorna Daniels were with them, when they had laughed and behaved like a happy family.

She set the tray on the table and poured the tea. The scent of bergamot in the Earl Grey rose with the steam. She added slices of lemon and handed a cup to Robbie.

'Thanks,' he said without enthusiasm.

Anna bit her lip. Despite her concern, despite her maternal instincts to protect her son, she had an irrational desire to slap him. Then it suddenly occurred to her that he might know more about Rachel's motives for harming them than he was saying and that that was what was troubling him. She had, after all, spoken to him at length before she attacked him. Robbie had let that slip not long after he had recovered from the anaesthetic. Perhaps he hadn't meant to. 'Did Rachel tell you why she hates us so much?' Anna asked as she picked her own cup up with a shaking hand.

'No. She just talked a lot of nonsense. It's obvious she's round the bend. The police seem to think she is. I don't know why I didn't see it before.'

'Robbie, please be truthful with me. Is there something I ought to know about?' She knew he was lying by the way in which he refused to look at her.

'There's nothing to tell you.' He lay back and closed his eyes.

Right, Anna thought. There's only one thing left to do. 'I'm going into Rickenham, I've got a couple of things to see to. I'll see you later.'

Robbie nodded but didn't speak. Once he'd have offered to go for her or at least show some interest in what she was doing. Anna wondered if he needed medical help and if she could persuade him to seek it.

She got her bag and a jacket because the air had become humid and sultry and it seemed likely there might be a summer storm. She waved to the man who came to cut the grass and do the heavy work in the garden and hoped Robbie would remember to pay him. She had put the money in an envelope in the kitchen. There were a few bits of shopping she needed but that could wait until after she had spoken to one of the detectives she had recently come to know.

In the underground car park she drove around for several minutes until she found an empty space then bought a ticket from the machine. It was as if she was watching herself. She was light-headed with the thought of what she might hear. On the other side of the plate-glass doors which were wedged open she approached the desk, gave her name and asked to speak to someone on DCI Roper's team.

'About what, madam?'

Anna was momentarily surprised until she remembered that not everyone would know about the horrors they had been through. She explained the situation briefly then waited while the desk sergeant made an internal call. A few minutes later Detective Sergeant Osborne came down the stairs looking reassuringly fresh and with a welcoming smile. The Chief was right, she thought, Anna Pearce wanted to hear the truth. 'Come with me, there's an empty room we can use.' Brenda inhaled deeply as she led the way. This wasn't going to be easy no matter how she put it. She had hoped not to have to break this news, that Robbie would have already done so, but the task was now hers. 'Would you like some tea or coffee?' she asked when they reached a small office.

'No thank you. I'm fine.'

'Have a seat, Anna.' They both sat down. Brenda clasped her hands together and rested them on the desk. 'How can I help you?'

'It's Robbie. I'm no expert but he seems

terribly depressed. I think he knows something that I don't and he doesn't want to tell me. Would you happen to know what it is?' Anna licked her lips. Her mouth was suddenly dry. 'If I knew what it was, it might help me to try to help Robbie.'

Brenda picked up a biro although she had no intention of writing anything. 'What I'm about to say will come as a shock. I think it may be what's upsetting Robbie, although I believe he's trying to protect you, Anna.'

'Protect me?' She had imagined she was protecting him. What was coming? What could be worse than what she had been going through?

Keeping her voice as neutral as possible Brenda said, 'John, your husband, was leading a double life. He spent time with a woman in London and had been doing so for many years. Her name was Paula Bowden.' She paused to let Anna work out the implications for herself. It seemed kinder than simply blurting out that Rachel Bowden was her husband's daughter.

'I see.' She laughed slightly hysterically. 'My God, it was going on for all those years and I never suspected a thing. What a fool I must have been.' Tears filled her eyes but she brushed them away with the back of her hand.

'There was no reason for you to have suspected anything, not if he was away so

260

often. And I'm sure he loved you.' It was a ridiculous platitude. There was no way she could have known if he had and she'd never even met the man but it was the best she could come up with.

'Yes, I'm sure he did love me, odd as that may seem. He was a kind and generous and loving man, he'd have had enough love to share with two women.'

'Paula didn't know John was dead. For the last few years of her life she believed he had abandoned her in favour of you, as did Rachel when she knew the truth. You see, Rachel wasn't aware of your or Robbie's existence until the day before her mother died. She wanted revenge for the deception both parents had carried out over the years.' Brenda hoped that if Anna learned how much the other woman had suffered by believing herself abandoned, she would find it easier to come to terms with the deception which had been practised upon her.

Anna blew her nose. She did not feel like Rachel Bowden, full of hatred and a desire for vengeance, she felt somehow relieved. John had presumably been happy and this somehow atoned for her many refusals to travel abroad with him. She had been too much of a home-maker, too selfish, perhaps, to comply with his wishes. She had concentrated instead on carving out her own life and bringing up her son. Whatever John had done, the marriage had worked. It had suited them both. But poor, poor Robbie, to have been taken in like that by his half-sister, to have slept with her and to now know that she had been laughing at him all the time. 'No wonder he wouldn't tell me, he must feel so ashamed.'

'He has no reason to be. He didn't know.'

Anna stood. 'Thank you for being so honest with me. I feel better now I know and I appreciate this wasn't easy for you. It's ironical, really, considering Rachel was responsible for her death, but I'm so glad my mother never knew about this. She adored John. Unless you have any more surprises for me it's time I faced Robbie.'

Brenda shook her head. 'There's nothing else. I'll show you out.'

Anna walked up to the supermarket at the top of the High Street. It was strange to be doing something as normal as picking up a basket and wandering along the aisles after learning that her husband had had a second family, but life must go on even if it meant reassessing the past. She knew that once she had done that she would have the strength to put it behind her. Hopefully Robbie would be able to do so too.

By the time she came to pay for the groceries she had made a decision. She would marry Phillip as soon as was practically possible. The past weeks had shown her that you could never know what was around the corner; happiness should be snatched the moment an opportunity arose. Robbie was young but she hoped he would accept this and get on with his life.

He was watching television when she returned. Anna switched off the set and stood in front of it. 'I know,' she said. 'I went to the police and they told me about your father. You should have told me, Robbie, we could have discussed it together, shared the burden, if you like. Anyway, it's out in the open now.'

He stared at her, shocked. 'You don't seem very upset.'

'I was, but I'm not now. It's in the past. At the risk of upsetting you further, tonight I'm going to tell Phillip I'm ready to marry him.' She watched his face. There was a flicker of pain before he smiled.

'I'm glad. It's about time. It's not right watching one's parent cohabiting.'

Anna smiled back as he got up and hugged her. It was their first physical contact for some time. She knew then that one day Robbie would become as carefree as he once had been.

'How did she take it?' Ian asked as they stood at the bar of the Three Feathers. The side doors were open but there was no breeze to freshen the place. The doors led to a paved area where a few wooden tables were arranged at right-angles. Against the walls were pots of flowers which were dying through neglect. It was stifling in the pub so they decided to take their drinks outside.

'With a great deal of equanimity,' Brenda replied as she followed him across the room. Scruffy Short and Greg Grant were not far behind them. Brenda swung her legs over the side of the bench attached to the table and sat down. 'In fact, I wondered afterwards if she had suspected something but had no wish to disturb the nice life she'd made for herself. He was away more than he was at home, which is enough to make anyone wonder if something was going on.'

'Not all men are like that. I'm certainly not.'

Brenda grinned. 'I know. And neither am I, but you know what I mean. Honestly, just look at him.'

Ian looked over his shoulder as a shadow fell over him. Short was approaching, in one hand a packet of crisps and in the other a pint of Guinness from which he was already taking a sip and spilling some down his shirt front.

Short winked at her. 'Admiring my Adonis-like body, are you, my lovely?'

'As if anyone possibly could.'

'That's no way to speak to a superior

officer. Shift up and make room, there's a good girl.' He and Greg sat down. 'I ought to put you across my knee and spank you, but then, you probably like that sort of thing.'

Unexpectedly Brenda laughed. Short looked in the direction she was now facing and saw why. Andrew Osborne had joined them unnoticed and had obviously heard his comment. 'Well, does she?' Short asked him, unabashed.

'Oh, you'd be surprised at some of her preferences,' he replied as he placed his own drink on the table and found a rusting chair to sit on.

Ian watched the interaction. His team got on well, which was fortunate as they spent so much time together, but it was nice that they also accepted Andrew who, being a solicitor, could be considered to be the opposition. However, he dealt mainly with personal injury cases so their paths rarely crossed in court. And they accepted him because they liked Brenda. Ian was gradually learning not to refer to him as the ugly brute and to see the man's good qualities and how much he loved his wife. Osborne had helped to smooth away the edge of defensiveness Brenda had carried around with her. And there was Greg, quietly talking to Andrew. Ian had yet to find out what made him tick but that would come in time. For the moment all that mattered was that he was gradually getting over his grief. And Short... Well, it looked as if they were stuck with him. Superintendent Thorne glossed over the matter if Ian asked how long his temporary post was supposed to last.

When their glasses were empty, feeling magnanimous, Ian offered to buy another round. He ignored the jibes this produced. It had become a standing joke that he was always the last to put his hand in his pocket but he'd never been able to work out why this was. Perhaps he drank more slowly than the others but he was certain he bought as many drinks as everyone else. With a cheerful grin he went back inside just as the first clap of thunder boomed in the distance and the others got up to follow him.

The summer would soon be over. Mark and Yvette were due to arrive at the weekend and he had yet to discuss their own holiday plans with Moira. How pleasant it was to be able to think about such mundane matters without work overshadowing them although, as he knew, other cases would soon prevent him doing so. 'Look, why don't I give Moira a ring and we'll make a night of it? We could all go and have something to eat.'

Brenda looked at Andrew and shrugged. As long as he was with her she didn't mind.

An hour later the six of them were seated at a round table in a Chinese restaurant with bowls of food in front of them. Outside a siren screamed as a police car tore down the road. It was quickly followed by a second. But for the moment they were off duty and determined to enjoy themselves. Like Anna Pearce they had long since learned that in their line of work it was foolish to live in any other way.

The publishers hope that this book has given you enjoyable reading. Large Print Books are especially designed to be as easy to see and hold as possible. If you wish a complete list of our books please ask at your local library or write directly to:

Magna Large Print Books
Magna House, Long Preston,
Skipton, North Yorkshire.
BD23 4ND

This Large Print Book, for people
who cannot read normal print,
is published under the auspices of

THE ULVERSCROFT FOUNDATION